A Dog of Flanders

AND OTHER STORIES

By

LOUISE DE LA RAMÉE

(OUIDA)

Illustrations by

MARIANO LEONE

Companion Library

GROSSET AND DUNLAP
PUBLISHERS
NEW YORK

Within the case were notes for two thousand francs

A Dog of Flanders

AND OTHER STORIES

The appealing story of an imaginative little boy, a loving old man, and a great faithful dog, all living together in poverty and love, has been a favorite for many years.

The "Nürnberg Stove," another of the stories in this book, is equally well loved by children everywhere. This tale centers around the magnificent stove of colored tile which warmed the hearts as well as the underfed little bodies of the Strehla children. How, in the end, the stove brought them all great happiness is a delightful and inspiring story.

CONTENTS

ILLUSTRATIONS

A DOG OF FLANDERS

*He kneeled down in the rank grass and surveyed the dog
with kindly eyes of pity*

A DOG OF FLANDERS

Nello and patrasche were left all alone in the world.

They were friends in a friendship closer than brotherhood. Nello was a little Ardennois—Patrasche was a big Fleming. They were both of the same age by length of years, yet one was still young, and the other was already old. They had dwelt together almost all their days: both were orphaned and destitute, and owed their lives to the same hand. It had been the beginning of the tie between them, their first bond of sympathy; and it had strengthened day by day, and had grown with their growth, firm and indissoluble, until they loved one another very greatly.

Their home was a little hut on the edge of a little village—a Flemish village a league from Antwerp, set amidst flat breadths of pasture and corn lands, with long lines of poplars and of alders bending in the breeze on the edge of the great canal which ran through it. It had about a score of houses and homesteads, with shutters of bright green or sky-blue, and roofs rose-red or black and white, and walls whitewashed until they shone in the sun like snow. In the center of the village stood a windmill, placed on a little moss-grown slope: it was a landmark to all the level country round. It had once been painted scarlet, sails and all, but that had been in its infancy, half a century or more earlier, when it had ground wheat for the soldiers of Napoleon; and it was now a ruddy brown, tanned by wind and weather. It went queerly by fits and starts, as though rheumatic and stiff in the joints from age, but it served the whole neighborhood, which would have thought it almost as impious to carry grain elsewhere as to attend any other religious service than the mass that was performed at the altar of the little old gray church, with its conical steeple, which stood opposite to it, and whose single bell rang morning, noon, and night with that strange, subdued, hollow sadness which every bell that hangs in the Low Countries seems to gain as an integral part of its melody.

Within sound of the little melancholy clock almost from their birth upward, they had dwelt together, Nello and Patrasche, in the little hut on the edge of the village, with the cathedral spire of Antwerp rising in the northeast, beyond the great green plain of seeding grass and spreading corn that stretched away from them like a tideless, changeless sea. It was the hut of a very old man, of a very poor man—of old Jehan Daas, who in his time had been a soldier, and who remembered the wars that had trampled the country as oxen tread down the furrows, and who had brought from his service nothing except a wound, which had made him a cripple.

When old Jehan Daas had reached his full eighty, his daughter had died in the Ardennes, hard by Stavelot, and had left him in legacy her two-year-old son. The old man could ill contrive to support himself, but he took up the additional burden uncomplainingly, and it soon became welcome and precious to him. Little Nello—which was but a pet diminutive for Nicolas—throve with him, and the old man and the little child lived in the poor little hut contentedly.

It was a very humble little mud hut indeed, but it was clean and white as a sea shell, and stood in a small plot of garden ground that yielded beans and herbs and pumpkins. They were very poor, terribly poor—many a day they had nothing at all to eat. They never by any chance had enough: to have had enough to eat would have been to have reached paradise at once. But the old man was very gentle and good to the boy, and the boy was a beautiful, innocent, truthful, tender-natured creature; and they were happy on a crust and a few leaves of cabbage, and asked no more of earth or heaven; save indeed that Patrasche should be always with them, since without Patrasche where would they have been?

For Patrasche was their alpha and omega; their treasury and granary; their store of gold and wand of wealth; their breadwinner and minister; their only friend and comforter. Patrasche dead or gone from them, they must have laid themselves down and died likewise. Patrasche was body, brains, hands, head, and feet to both of them: Patrasche was their very life, their very soul. For Jehan Daas was old and a cripple, and Nello was but a child; and Patrasche was their dog.

A dog of Flanders—yellow of hide, large of head and limb, with wolf-like ears that stood erect, and legs bowed and feet widened in the muscular development wrought in his breed by many generations of hard service. Patrasche came of a race which had toiled hard and cruelly from sire to son in Flanders many a century—slaves of slaves, dogs of the people, beasts of the shafts and the harness, creatures that lived straining their sinews in the gall of the cart, and died breaking their hearts on the flints of the streets.

Patrasche had been born of parents who had labored hard all their days over the sharp-set stones of the various cities and the long, shadowless, weary roads of the two Flanders and of Brabant. He had been born to no other heritage than those of pain and of toil. He had been fed on curses and baptized with blows. Before he was fully grown he had known the bitter gall of the cart and the collar. Before he had entered his thirteenth month he had become the property of a hardware dealer, who was accustomed to wander over the land north and south, from the blue sea to the green mountains. They sold him for a small price, because he was too young.

This man was a drunkard and a brute. The life of Patrasche was a life of hell. His purchaser was a sullen, ill-living, brutal Brabantois, who heaped his cart full with pots and pans and flagons and buckets, and other wares of crockery and brass and tin, and left Patrasche to draw the load as best he might, whilst he himself lounged idly by the side in fat and sluggish ease, smoking his black pipe and stopping at every wine shop or café on the road.

Happily for Patrasche—or unhappily—he was very strong: he came of an iron race, long born and bred to such cruel travail; so that he did not die, but managed to drag on a wretched existence under the brutal burdens. One day, after two years of this long and deadly agony, Patrasche was going on as usual along one of the straight, dusty, unlovely roads that lead to the city of Rubens. It was full midsummer, and very warm. His cart was very heavy, piled high with goods in metal and in earthenware. His owner sauntered on without noticing him otherwise than by the crack of the whip as it curled round his quivering loins. The Brabantois had paused to drink beer himself at every wayside house, but he had forbidden Patrasche to stop a moment for a draught from the canal. Going along thus, in the full sun, on a scorching highway, having eaten nothing for twenty-four hours, and, which was far worse to him, not having tasted water for near twelve, being blind with dust, sore with blows, and stupefied with the merciless weight which dragged upon his loins, Patrasche, for once, staggered and foamed a little at the mouth, and fell.

He fell in the middle of the white dusty road, in the full glare of the sun; he was sick unto death, and motionless. His master gave him the only medicine in his pharmacy—kicks and oaths and blows with a cudgel of oak, which had been often the only food and drink, the only wage and reward, ever offered to him. But Patrasche was beyond the reach of any torture or of any curses. Patrasche lay, dead to all appearances, down in the white powder of the summer dust. After a while, finding it useless to assail his ribs with punishment and his ears with maledictions, the Brabantois—deeming life gone in him, or going so nearly that his carcass was forever useless, unless indeed someone should strip it of the skin for gloves—cursed him fiercely in farewell, struck off the leathern bands of the harness, kicked his body heavily aside into the grass, and, groaning and muttering in savage wrath, pushed the cart lazily along the road uphill, and left the dying dog there for the ants to sting and for the crows to pick.

It was the last day before Kermesse away at Louvain, and the Brabantois was in haste to reach the fair and get a good place for his truck of brass wares. He was in fierce wrath, because Patrasche had been a strong and much-enduring animal, and because he himself had now the hard task of pushing his charette all the way to Louvain. But to stay to look after Patrasche never entered his thoughts: the beast was dying and useless, and he would steal, to replace him, the first large dog that he found wandering alone out of sight of its master. Patrasche had cost him nothing, or next to nothing, and for two long, cruel years he had made him toil ceaselessly in his service from sunrise to sunset, through summer and winter, in fair weather and foul.

He had got a fair use and a good profit out of Patrasche: being human, he was wise, and left the dog to draw his last breath alone in the ditch, and have his bloodshot eyes plucked out as they might be by the birds, while he himself went on his way to beg and to steal, to eat and to drink, to dance and to sing, in the mirth at Louvain. A dying dog, a dog of the cart—why should he waste hours over its agonies at peril of losing a handful of copper coins, at peril of a shout of laughter?

Patrasche lay there, flung in the grass-green ditch. It was a busy road that day, and hundreds of people, on foot and on mules, in wagons or in carts, went by, tramping quickly and joyously on to Louvain. Some saw him, most did not even look: all passed on. A dead dog more or less—it was nothing in Brabant: it would be nothing anywhere in the world.

After a time, among the holiday makers, there came a little old man who was bent and lame, and very feeble. He was in no guise for feasting: he was very poorly and miserably clad, and he dragged his silent way slowly through the dust among the pleasure seekers. He looked at Patrasche, paused, wondered, turned aside, then kneeled down in the rank grass and weeds of the ditch, and surveyed the dog with kindly eyes of pity. There was with him a little rosy, fair-haired, dark-eyed child of a few years old, who pattered in amidst the bushes, that were for him breast-high, and stood gazing with a pretty serious-ness upon the poor, great, quiet beast.

Thus it was that these two first met—the little Nello and the big Patrasche.

The upshot of that day was, that old Jehan Daas, with much laborious effort, drew the sufferer homeward to his own little hut, which was a stone's throw off amidst the fields, and there tended him with so much care that the sickness, which had been a brain seizure, brought on by heat and thirst and exhaustion, with time and shade and rest passed away, and health and strength returned, and Patrasche staggered up again upon his four stout, tawny legs.

Now for many weeks he had been useless, powerless, sore, near to death; but all this time he had heard no rough word, had felt no harsh touch, but only the pitying murmurs of the little child's voice and the soothing caress of the old man's hand.

In his sickness they too had grown to care for him, this lonely old man and the little happy child. He had a corner of the hut, with a heap of dry grass for his bed; and they had learned to listen eagerly for his breathing in the dark night, to tell them that he lived; and when he first was well enough to essay a loud, hollow, broken bay, they laughed aloud, and almost wept together for joy at such a sign of his sure restoration; and little Nello, in delighted glee, hung round his rugged neck chains of marguerites, and kissed him with fresh and ruddy lips.

So then, when Patrasche arose, himself again, strong, big, gaunt, powerful, his great wistful eyes had a gentle astonishment in them that there were no curses to rouse him and no blows to drive him; and his heart awakened to a mighty love, which never wavered once in its fidelity while life abode with him.

But Patrasche, being a dog, was grateful. Patrasche lay pondering long with grave, tender, musing brown eyes, watching the movements of his friends.

Now, the old soldier, Jehan Daas, could do nothing for his living but limp about a little with a small cart, with which he carried daily the milk cans of those happier neighbors who owned cattle away into the town of Antwerp. The villagers gave him the employment a little out of charity—more because it suited them well to send their milk into the town by so honest a carrier, and bide at home themselves to look after their gardens, their cows, their poultry, or their little fields. But it was becoming hard work for the old man. He was eighty-three, and Antwerp was a good league off, or more.

Patrasche watched the milk cans come and go that one day when he had got well and was lying in the sun with the wreath of marguerites round his tawny neck.

The next morning, Patrasche, before the old man had touched the cart, arose and walked to it and placed himself betwixt its handles, and testified as plainly as dumb show could do his desire and his ability to work in return for the bread of charity that he had eaten. Jehan Daas resisted long, for the old man was one of those who thought it a foul shame to bind dogs to labor for which Nature never formed them. But Patrasche would not be gainsaid: finding they did not harness him, he tried to draw the cart onward with his teeth.

At length Jehan Daas gave way, vanquished by the persistence and the gratitude of this creature whom he had succored. He fashioned his cart so that Patrasche could run in it, and this he did every morning of his life thenceforward.

When the winter came, Jehan Daas thanked the blessed fortune that had brought him to the dying dog in the ditch that fair-day of Louvain; for he was very old, and he grew feebler with each year, and he would ill have known how to pull his load of milk cans over the snows and through the deep ruts in the mud if it had not been for the strength and the industry of the animal he had befriended. As for Patrasche, it seemed heaven to him. After the frightful burdens that his old master had compelled him to strain under, at the call of the whip at every step, it seemed nothing to him but amusement to step out with this little light green cart, with its bright brass cans, by the side of the gentle old man who always paid him with a tender caress and with a kindly word. Besides, his work was over by three or four in the day, and after that time he was free to do as he would—to stretch himself, to sleep in the sun, to wander in the fields, to romp with the young child, or to play with his fellow dogs. Patrasche was very happy.

Fortunately for his peace, his former owner was killed in a drunken brawl at the Kermesse of Mechlin, and so sought not after him nor disturbed him in his new and well-loved home.

A few years later, old Jehan Daas, who had always been a cripple, became so paralyzed with rheumatism that it was impossible for him to go out with the cart any more. Then little Nello, being now grown to his sixth year of age, and knowing the town well from having accompanied his grandfather so many times, took his place beside the cart, and sold the milk and received the coins in exchange, and brought them back to their respective owners with a pretty grace and seriousness which charmed all who beheld him.

The little Ardennois was a beautiful child, with dark,

grave, tender eyes, and a lovely bloom upon his face, and fair locks that clustered to his throat; and many an artist sketched the group as it went by him—the green cart with the brass flagons of Teniers and Mieris and Van Tal, and the great tawny-colored, massive dog, with his belled harness that chimed cheerily as he went, and the small figure that ran beside him which had little white feet in great wooden shoes, and a soft, grave, innocent, happy face like the little fair children of Rubens.

Nello and Patrasche did the work so well and so joyfully together that Jehan Daas himself, when the summer came and he was better again, had no need to stir out, but could sit in the doorway in the sun and see them go forth through the garden wicket, and then doze and dream and pray a little, and then awake again as the clock tolled three and watch for their return. And on their return Patrasche would shake himself free of his harness with a bay of glee, and Nello would recount with pride the doings of the day; and they would all go in together to their meal of rye bread and milk or soup, and would see the shadows lengthen over the great plain, and see the twilight veil the fair cathedral spire; and then lie down together to sleep peacefully while the old man said a prayer.

So the days and the years went on, and the lives of Nello and Patrasche were very happy and innocent and healthful.

In the spring and summer especially were they glad. Flanders is not a lovely land, and around the burgh of Rubens it is perhaps least lovely of all. Corn and colza, pasture and plow, succeed each other on the characterless plain in wearying repetition, and save by some gaunt gray tower, with its peal of pathetic bells, or some figure coming athwart the fields, made picturesque by a gleaner's bundle or a woodman's fagot, there is no change, no variety, no beauty anywhere; and he who has dwelt upon the mountains or amidst the forest feels oppressed as by imprisonment with the tedium and the needlessness of that vast and dreary level. But it is green and very fertile, and it has wide horizons that have a certain charm of their own even in their dullness and monotony; and among the rushes by the waterside the flowers grow, and the trees rise tall and fresh where the barges glide with their great hulks black against the sun, and their little green barrels and vari-colored flags gay against the leaves. Anyway, there is greenery and breadth of space enough to be as good as beauty to a child and a dog; and these two asked no better, when their work was done, than to lie buried in the lush grasses on the side of the canal, and watch the cumbrous vessels drifting by and bringing the crisp salt smell of the sea among the blossoming scents of the country summer.

True, in the winter it was harder, and they had to rise in the darkness and the bitter cold, and they had seldom as much as they could have eaten any day, and the hut was scarce better than a shed when the nights were cold, although it looked so pretty in warm weather, buried in a great kindly clambering vine, that never bore fruit, indeed, but which covered it with luxuriant green tracery all through the months of blossom and harvest. In winter the winds found many holes in the walls of the poor little hut, and the vine was black and leafless, and the bare lands looked very bleak and drear without, and sometimes within the floor was flooded and then frozen. In winter it was hard, and the snow numbed the little white limbs of Nello, and the icicles cut the brave untiring feet of Patrasche.

But even then they were never heard to lament, either

of them.   The child's wooden shoes and the dog's four legs would trot manfully together over the frozen fields to the chime of the bells on the harness; and then sometimes, in the streets of Antwerp, some housewife would bring them a bowl of soup and a handful of bread, or some kindly trader would throw some billets of fuel into the little cart as it went homeward, or some woman in their own village would bid them keep some share of the milk they carried for their own food; and then they would run over the white lands, through the early darkness, bright and happy, and burst with a shout of joy into their home.

So, on the whole, it was well with them, very well; and Patrasche, meeting on the highway or in the public streets the many dogs who toiled from daybreak into nightfall, paid only with blows and curses, and loosened from the shafts with a kick to starve and freeze as best they might—Patrasche in his heart was very grateful to his fate, and thought it the fairest and the kindliest the world could hold.   Though he was often very hungry indeed when he lay down at night; though he had to work in the heats of summer noons and the rasping chills of winter dawns; though his feet were often tender with wounds from the sharp edges of the jagged pavement; though he had to perform tasks beyond his strength and against his nature—yet he was grateful and content: he did his duty with each day, and the eyes that he loved smiled down on him.   It was sufficient for Patrasche.

There was only one thing which caused Patrasche any uneasiness in his life, and it was this.   Antwerp, as all the world knows, is full at every turn of old piles of stones dark and ancient and majestic, standing in crooked courts, jammed against gateways and taverns, rising by the water's edge, with bells ringing above them in the air, and ever and again out of their arched doors a swell of music pealing. There they remain, the grand old sanctuaries of the past, shut in amidst the squalor, the hurry, the crowds, the unloveliness, and the commerce of the modern world, and all day long the clouds drift and the birds circle and the winds sigh around them, and beneath the earth at their feet there sleeps—RUBENS.

And the greatness of the mighty Master still rests upon Antwerp, and wherever we turn in its narrow streets his glory lies therein, so that all mean things are thereby transfigured; and as we pace slowly through the winding ways, and by the edge of the stagnant water, and through the noisome courts, his spirit abides with us, and the heroic beauty of his visions is about us, and the stones that once felt his footsteps and bore his shadow seem to arise and speak of him with living voices. For the city which is the tomb of Rubens still lives to us through him, and him alone.

It is so quiet there by that great white sepulcher—so quiet, save only when the organ peals and the choir cries aloud the Salve Regina or the Kyrie Eleison. Sure no artist ever had a greater gravestone than that pure marble sanctuary gives to him in the heart of his birthplace in the chancel of St. Jacques.

Without Rubens, what were Antwerp? A dirty, dusky, bustling mart, which no man would ever care to look upon save the traders who do business on its wharves. With Rubens, to the whole world of men it is a sacred name, a sacred soil, a Bethlehem where a god of Art saw light, a Golgotha where a god of Art lies dead.

O nations closely should you treasure your great men, for by them alone will the future know of you. Flanders in her generations has been wise. In his life she glorified this greatest of her sons, and in his death she magnifies his name. But her wisdom is very rare.

Now, the trouble of Patrasche was this. Into these great, sad piles of stones, that reared their melancholy majesty above the crowded roofs, the child Nello would many and many a time enter, and disappear through their dark arched portals, whilst Patrasche, left without upon the pavement, would wearily and vainly ponder on what could be the charm which thus allured from him his inseparable and beloved companion. Once or twice he did essay to see for himself, clattering up the steps with his milk-cart behind him; but thereon he had been always sent back again summarily by a tall custodian in black clothes and silver chains of office; and fearful of bringing his little master into trouble, he desisted, and remained couched patiently before the churches until such time as the boy reappeared. It was not the fact of his going into them which disturbed Patrasche: he knew that people went to church: all the village went to the small, tumble-down, gray pile opposite the red windmill. What troubled him was that little Nello always looked strangely when he came out, always very flushed or very pale; and whenever he returned home after such visitations would sit silent and dreaming, not caring to play, but gazing out at the evening skies beyond the line of the canal, very subdued and almost sad.

What was it: wondered Patrasche. He thought it could not be good or natural for the little lad to be so grave, and in his dumb fashion he tried all he could to keep Nello by him in the sunny fields or in the busy market place. But to the churches Nello would go: most often of all would he go to the great cathedral; and Patrasche, left without on the stones by the iron fragments of Quentin Matsys's gate, would stretch himself and yawn and sigh, and even howl now and then, all in vain, until the doors closed and the child perforce came forth again, and winding his arms about the dog's neck would kiss him on his broad, tawny-colored forehead, and murmur always the same words: "If I could only see them, Patrasche!—if I could only see them!"

What were they? pondered Patrasche, looking up with large, wistful, sympathetic eyes.

One day, when the custodian was out of the way and the doors left ajar, he got in for a moment after his little friend and saw. "They" were two great covered pictures on either side of the choir.

Nello was kneeling, rapt as in an ecstasy, before the altar picture of the Assumption, and when he noticed Patrasche, and rose and drew the dog gently out into the air, his face was wet with tears, and he looked up at the veiled places as he passed them, and murmured to his companion, "It is so terrible not to see them, Patrasche, just because one is poor and cannot pay. He never meant that the poor should not see them when he painted them, I am sure. He would have had us see them any day, every day: that I am sure. And they keep them shrouded there—shrouded in the dark, the beautiful things!—and they never feel the light, and no eyes look on them, unless rich people come and pay. If I could only see them, I would be content to die."

But he could not see them, and Patrasche could not help him, for to gain the silver piece that the church exacts as the price for looking on the glories of the Elevation of the Cross and the Descent of the Cross was a thing as utterly beyond the powers of either of them as it would have been to scale the heights of the cathedral spire. They had never so much as a sou to spare: if they cleared enough to get a little wood for the stove, a little broth for the pot, it was the utmost they could do. And yet the heart of the child was set in sore and endless longing upon beholding the greatness of the two veiled Rubens.

The whole soul of the little Ardennois thrilled and stirred with an absorbing passion for Art. Going on his ways through the old city in the early days before the sun or the people had risen, Nello, who looked only a little peasant boy, with a great dog drawing milk to sell from door to door, was in a heaven of dreams whereof Rubens was the god. Nello, cold and hungry, with stockingless feet in wooden shoes, and the winter winds blowing among his curls and lifting his poor thin garments, was in a rapture of meditation, wherein all that he saw was the beautiful fair face of the Mary of the Assumption, with the waves of her golden hair lying upon her shoulders, and the light of an eternal sun shining down upon her brow. Nello, reared in poverty, and buffeted by fortune, and untaught in letters and unheeded by men, had the compensation or the curse which is called Genius.

No one knew it. He as little as any. No one knew it. Only indeed Patrasche, who, being with him always, saw him draw with chalk upon the stones any and every thing that grew or breathed, heard him on his little bed of hay murmur all manner of timid, pathetic prayers to the spirit of the great Master; watched his gaze darken and his face radiate at the evening glow of sunset or the rosy rising of the dawn; and felt many and many a time the tears of a strange, nameless pain and joy, mingled together, fall hotly from the bright young eyes upon his own wrinkled yellow forehead.

"I should go to my grave quite content if I thought, Nello, that when thou growest a man thou couldst own this hut and the little plot of ground, and labor for thyself,

and be called Baas by thy neighbors," said the old man
Jehan many an hour from his bed. For to own a bit of
soil, and to be called Baas—master—by the hamlet
round, is to have achieved the highest ideal of a Flemish
peasant; and the old soldier, who had wandered over all
the earth in his youth, and had brought nothing back,
deemed in his old age that to live and die on one spot in
contented humility was the fairest fate he could desire for
his darling. But Nello said nothing.

The same leaven was working in him that in other
times begat Rubens and Jordaens and the Van Eycks, and
all their wondrous tribe, and in times more recent begat in
the green country of the Ardennes, where the Meuse
washes the old walls of Dijon, the great artist of the
Patroclus, whose genius is too near us for us aright to
measure its divinity.

Nello dreamed of other things in the future than of
tilling the little rood of earth, and living under the wattle
roof, and being called Baas by neighbors a little poorer or
a little less poor than himself. The cathedral spire, where
it rose beyond the fields in the ruddy evening skies or in
the dim, gray misty mornings, said other things to him
than this. But these he told only to Patrasche, whisper-
ing, childlike, his fancies in the dog's ear when they went
together at their work through the fogs of the daybreak,
or lay together at their rest among the rustling rushes by
the water's side.

For such dreams are not easily shaped into speech to
awake the slow sympathies of human auditors; and they
would only have sorely perplexed and troubled the poor
old man bedridden in his corner, who, for his part,
whenever he had trodden the streets of Antwerp, had
thought the daub of blue and red that they called a
Madonna, on the walls of the wine-shop where he drank

his sou's worth of black beer, quite as good as any of the famous altarpieces for which the stranger folk traveled far and wide into Flanders from every land on which the good sun shone.

There was only one other beside Patrasche to whom Nello could talk at all of his daring fantasies. This other was little Alois, who lived at the old red mill on the grassy mound, and whose father, the miller, was the best-to-do husbandman in all the village. Little Alois was only a pretty baby with soft, round, rosy features made lovely by those sweet dark eyes that the Spanish rule has left in so many a Flemish face, in testimony of the Alvan dominion, as Spanish art has left broadsown throughout the country majestic palaces and stately courts, gilded house fronts and sculptured lintels—histories in blazonry and poems in stone.

Little Alois was often with Nello and Patrasche. They played in the fields, they ran in the snow, they gathered the daisies and bilberries, they went up to the old gray church together, and they often sat together by the broad wood fire in the millhouse. Little Alois, indeed, was the richest child in the hamlet. She had neither brother nor sister; her blue serge dress had never a hole in it; at Kermesse she had as many gilded nuts and Agni Dei in sugar as her hands could hold; and when she went up for her first communion her flaxen curls were covered with a cap of richest Mechlin lace, which had been her mother's and her grandmother's before it came to her. Men spoke already, though she had but twelve years, of the good wife she would be for their sons to woo and win; but she herself was a little gay, simple child, in nowise conscious of her heritage, and she loved no playfellows so well as Jehan Daas's grandson and his dog.

One day her father, Baas Cogez, a good man, but

somewhat stern, came on a pretty group in the long meadow behind the mill, where the aftermath had that day been cut. It was his little daughter sitting amidst the hay with the great tawny head of Patrasche on her lap, many wreaths of poppies and blue cornflowers round them both: on a clean smooth slab of pine wood the boy Nello drew their likeness with a stick of charcoal.

The miller stood and looked at the portrait with tears in his eyes, it was so strangely like, and he loved his only child closely and well. Then he roughly chid the little girl for idling there while her mother needed her within, and sent her indoors crying and afraid: then, turning, he snatched the wood from Nello's hands. "Dost do much of such folly?" he asked, but there was a tremble in his voice.

Nello colored and hung his head. "I draw everything I see," he murmured.

The miller was silent: then he stretched his hand out with a franc in it. "It is folly, as I say, and evil waste of time: nevertheless, it is like Alois, and will please the housemother. Take this silver bit for it and leave it for me."

The color died out of the face of the young Ardennois; he lifted his head and put his hands behind his back. "Keep your money and the portrait both, Baas Cogez," he said, simply. "You have been often good to me." Then he called Patrasche to him, and walked away across the field.

"I could have seen them with that franc," he murmured to Patrasche, "but I could not sell her picture—not even for them."

Baas Cogez went into his millhouse sore troubled in his mind. "That lad must not be so much with Alois," he said to his wife that night. "Trouble may come of it hereafter: he is fifteen now, and she is twelve; and the boy is comely of face and form."

"And he is a good lad and a loyal," said the housewife feasting her eyes on the piece of pine wood where it was throned above the chimney with a cuckoo clock in oak and a Calvary in wax.

"Yea, I do not gainsay that," said the miller, draining his pewter flagon.

"Then, if what you think of were ever to come to pass," said the wife, hesitatingly, "would it matter so much? She will have enough for both, and one cannot be better than happy."

"You are a woman, and therefore a fool," said the miller, harshly, striking his pipe on the table. "The lad is naught but a beggar, and, with these painter's fancies, worse than a beggar. Have a care that they are not together in the future, or I will send the child to the surer keeping of the nuns of the Sacred Heart."

The poor mother was terrified, and promised humbly to do his will. Not that she could bring herself altogether to separate the child from her favorite playmate, nor did the miller even desire that extreme of cruelty to a young lad who was guilty of nothing except poverty. But there were many ways in which little Alois was kept away from her chosen companion: and Nello, being a boy proud and quiet and sensitive, was quickly wounded, and ceased to turn his own steps and those of Patrasche, as he had been used to do with every moment of leisure, to the old red mill upon the slope. What his offense was he did not know: he supposed he had in some manner angered Baas Cogez by taking the portrait of Alois in the meadow; and when the child who loved him would run to him and nestle her hand in his, he would smile at her very sadly and say with tender concern for her before himself, "Nay,

*On a clean slab of pine wood, Nello drew their likeness
with a stick of charcoal*

Alois, do not anger your father. He thinks that I make you idle, dear, and he is not pleased that you should be with me. He is a good man and loves you well: we will not anger him, Alois."

But it was with a sad heart that he said it, and the earth did not look so bright to him as it had used to do when he went out at sunrise under the poplars down the straight roads with Patrasche. The old red mill had been a landmark to him, and he had been used to pause by it, going and coming, for a cheery greeting with its people as her little flaxen head rose above the low mill wicket, and her little rosy hands had held out a bone or a crust to Patrasche. Now the dog looked wistfully at a closed door, and the boy went on without pausing, with a pang at his heart, and the child sat within with tears dropping slowly on the knitting to which she was set on her little stool by the stove; and Baas Cogez, working among his sacks and his mill gear, would harden his will and say to himself, "It is best so. The lad is all but a beggar, and full of idle, dreaming fooleries. Who knows what mischief might not come of it in the future?" So he was wise in his generation, and would not have the door unbarred, except upon rare and formal occasions, which seemed to have neither warmth nor mirth in them to the two children, who had been accustomed so long to a daily gleeful, careless, happy interchange of greeting, speech, and pastime, with no other watcher of their sports or auditor of their fancies than Patrasche, sagely shaking the brazen bells of his collar and responding with all a dog's swift sympathies to their every change of mood.

All this while the little panel of pine wood remained over the chimney in the mill kitchen with the cuckoo clock and the waxen Calvary, and sometimes it seemed to

Nello a little hard that whilst his gift was accepted he himself should be denied.

But he did not complain: it was his habit to be quiet: old Jehan Daas had said ever to him, "We are poor: we must take what God sends—the ill with the good: the poor cannot choose."

To which the boy had always listened in silence, being reverent of his old grandfather; but nevertheless a certain vague, sweet hope, such as beguiles the children of genius, had whispered in his heart, "Yet the poor do choose sometimes—choose to be great, so that men cannot say them nay." And he thought so still in his innocence; and one day, when the little Alois, finding him by chance alone among the cornfields by the canal, ran to him and held him close, and sobbed piteously because the morrow would be her saint's day, and for the first time in all her life her parents had failed to bid him to the little supper and romp in the great barns with which her feast day was always celebrated, Nello had kissed her and murmured to her in firm faith, "It shall be different one day, Alois. One day that little bit of pine wood that your father has of mine shall be worth its weight in silver; and he will not shut the door against me then. Only love me always, dear little Alois, only love me always, and I will be great."

"And if I do not love you?" the pretty child asked, pouting a little through her tears, and moved by the instinctive coquetries of her sex.

Nello's eyes left her face and wandered to the distance, where in the red and gold of the Flemish night the cathedral spire rose. There was a smile on his face so sweet and yet so sad that little Alois was awed by it. "I will be great still," he said under his breath—"great still, or die, Alois."

"You do not love me," said the little spoilt child, pushing him away; but the boy shook his head and smiled, and went on his way through the tall yellow corn, seeing as in a vision some day in a fair future when he should come into that old familiar land and ask Alois of her people, and be not refused or denied, but received in honor, whilst the village folk should throng to look upon him and say in one another's ears, "Dost see him? He is a king among men, for he is a great artist and the world speaks his name; and yet he was only our poor little Nello, who was a beggar, as one may say, and only got his bread by the help of his dog." And he thought how he would fold his grandsire in furs and purples, and portray him as the old man is portrayed in the Family in the chapel of St. Jacques; and of how he would hang the throat of Patrasche with a collar of gold, and place him on his right hand, and say to the people, "This was once my only friend;" and of how he would build himself a great white marble palace, and make to himself luxuriant gardens of pleasure, on the slope looking outward to where the cathedral spire rose, and not dwell in it himself, but summon to it, as to a home, all men young and poor and friendless, but of the will to do mighty things; and of how he would say to them always, if they sought to bless his name, "Nay, do not thank me—thank Rubens. Without him, what should I have been?" And these dreams, beautiful, impossible, innocent, free of all selfishness, full of heroical worship, were so closely about him as he went that he was happy—happy even on this sad anniversary of Alois's saint's day, when he and Patrasche went home by themselves to the little dark hut and the meal of black bread, whilst in the millhouse all the children of the village sang and laughed, and ate the big round cakes of Dijon and the almond gingerbread of Brabant, and danced in the great barn to the light of the stars and the music of flute and fiddle.

"Never mind, Patrasche," he said, with his arms round the dog's neck as they both sat in the door of the hut, where the sounds of the mirth at the mill came down to them on the night air—"never mind. It shall all be changed by and by."

He believed in the future: Patrasche, of more experience and of more philosophy, thought that the loss of the mill supper in the present was ill compensated by dreams of milk and honey in some vague hereafter. And Patrasche growled whenever he passed by Baas Cogez.

"This is Alois's name-day, is it not?" said the old man Daas that night from the corner where he was stretched upon his bed of sacking.

The boy gave a gesture of assent: he wished that the old man's memory had erred a little, instead of keeping such sure account.

"And why not there?" his grandfather pursued. "Thou hast never missed a year before, Nello."

"Thou art too sick to leave," murmured the lad, bending his handsome young head over the bed.

"Tut! tut! Mother Nulette would have come and sat with me, as she does scores of times. What is the cause, Nello?" the old man persisted. "Thou surely hast not had ill words with the little one?"

"Nay, grandfather—never," said the boy quickly, with a hot color in his bent face. "Simply and truly, Baas Cogez did not have me asked this year. He has taken some whim against me."

"But thou hast done nothing wrong?"

"That I know—nothing. I took the portrait of Alois on a piece of pine: that is all."

"Ah!" The old man was silent: the truth suggested

itself to him with the boy's innocent answer. He was tied to a bed of dried leaves in the corner of a wattle hut, but he had not wholly forgotten what the ways of the world were like.

He drew Nello's fair head fondly to his breast with a tenderer gesture. "Thou art very poor, my child," he said with a quiver the more in his aged, trembling voice—"so poor! It is very hard for thee."

"Nay, I am rich," murmured Nello; and in his innocence he thought so—rich with the imperishable powers that are mightier than the might of kings. And he went and stood by the door of the hut in the quiet autumn night, and watched the stars troop by and the tall poplars bend and shiver in the wind. All the casements of the millhouse were lighted, and every now and then the notes of the flute came to him. The tears fell down his cheeks, for he was but a child, yet he smiled, for he said to himself, "In the future!" He stayed there until all was quite still and dark, and then he and Patrasche went within and slept together, long and deeply, side by side.

Now he had a secret which only Patrasche knew. There was a little outhouse to the hut, which no one entered but himself—a dreary place, but with abundant clear light from the north. Here he had fashioned himself rudely an easel in rough lumber, and here on a great gray sea of stretched paper he had given shape to one of the innumerable fancies which possessed his brain. No one had ever taught him anything; colors he had no means to buy; he had gone without bread many a time to procure even the few rude vehicles that he had here; and it was only in black or white that he could fashion the things he saw. This great figure which he had drawn here in chalk was only an old man sitting on a fallen tree—only that. He had seen old Michel the woodman sitting so at evening many a time. He had never had a soul to tell him of outline or perspective, of anatomy or of shadow, and yet he had given all the weary, worn-out age, all the sad, quiet patience, all the rugged, careworn pathos of his original, and given them so that the old lonely figure was a poem, sitting there, meditative and alone, on the dead tree, with the darkness of the descending night behind him.

It was rude of course, in a way, and had many faults, no doubt; and yet it was real, true in nature, true in art and very mournful, and in a manner beautiful.

Patrasche had lain quiet countless hours watching its gradual creation after the labor of each day was done, and he knew that Nello had a hope—vain and wild perhaps, but strongly cherished—of sending this great drawing to compete for a prize of two hundred francs a year which it was announced in Antwerp would be open to every lad of talent, scholar or peasant, under eighteen, who would attempt to win it with some unaided work of chalk or pencil. Three of the foremost artists in the town of Rubens were to be the judges and elect the victor according to his merits.

All the spring and summer and autumn Nello had been at work upon this treasure, which, if triumphant, would build him his first step toward independence and the mysteries of the art which he blindly, ignorantly, and yet passionately adored.

He said nothing to any one: his grandfather would not have understood, and little Alois was lost to him. Only to Patrasche he told all, and whispered, "Rubens would give it me, I think, if he knew."

Patrasche thought so too, for he knew that Rubens had loved dogs or he had never painted them with such exquisite fidelity; and men who loved dogs were, as Patrasche knew, always pitiful.

The drawings were to go in on the first day of December, and the decision be given on the twenty-fourth, so that he who should win might rejoice with all his people at the Christmas season.

In the twilight of a bitter wintry day, and with a beating heart, now quick with hope, now faint with fear Nello placed the great picture on his little green milk cart, and took it with the help of Patrasche, into the town. and there left it, as enjoined, at the doors of a public building.

"Perhaps it is worth nothing at all. How can I tell?" he thought, with the heartsickness of a great timidity. Now that he had left it there, it seemed to him so hazardous, so vain, so foolish, to dream that he, a little lad with bare feet, who barely knew his letters, could do anything at which great painters, real artists, could ever deign to look. Yet he took heart as he went by the cathedral: the lordly form of Rubens seemed to rise from the fog and the darkness, and to loom in its magnificence before him, whilst the lips, with their kindly smile, seemed to him to murmur, "Nay, have courage! It was not by a weak heart and by faint fears that I wrote my name for all time upon Antwerp."

Nello ran home through the cold night, comforted. He had done his best: the rest must be as God willed, he thought, in that innocent, unquestioning faith which had been taught him in the little gray chapel among the willows and the poplar trees.

The winter was very sharp already. That night, after they reached the hut, snow fell; and fell for very many days after that, so that the paths and the divisions in the fields were all obliterated, and all the smaller streams were frozen over, and the cold was intense upon the plains. Then, indeed, it became hard work to go round for the milk while the world was all dark, and carry it through the darkness to the silent town. Hard work, especially for Patrasche, for the passage of the years, that were only bringing Nello a stronger youth, were bringing him old age, and his joints were stiff and his bones ached often. But he would never give up his share of the labor. Nello would fain have spared him and drawn the cart himself, but Patrasche would not allow it. All he would ever permit or accept was the help of a thrust from behind to the truck as it lumbered along through the ice ruts. Patrasche had lived in harness, and he was proud of it. He suffered a great deal sometimes from frost, and the terrible roads, and the rheumatic pains of his limbs, but he only drew his breath hard and bent his stout neck, and trod onward with steady patience.

"Rest thee at home, Patrasche—it is time thou didst rest—and I can quite well push in the cart by myself," urged Nello many a morning; but Patrasche, who understood him aright, would no more have consented to stay at home than a veteran soldier to shirk when the charge was sounding; and every day he would rise and place himself in his shafts, and plod along over the snow through the fields that his four round feet had left their print upon so many, many years.

"One must never rest till one dies," thought Patrasche; and sometimes it seemed to him that that time of rest for him was not very far off. His sight was less clear than it had been, and it gave him pain to rise after the night's sleep, though he would never lie a moment in his straw when once the bell of the chapel tolling five let him know that the daybreak of labor had begun.

"My poor Patrasche, we shall soon lie quiet together, you and I," said old Jehan Daas, stretching out to stroke the head of Patrasche with the old withered hand which had always shared with him its one poor crust of bread;

and the hearts of the old man and the old dog ached together with one thought: When they were gone, who would care for their darling?

One afternoon, as they came back from Antwerp over the snow, which had become hard and smooth as marble over all the Flemish plains, they found dropped in the road a pretty little puppet, a tambourine-player, all scarlet and gold, about six inches high, and, unlike greater personages when Fortune lets them drop, quite unspoiled and unhurt by its fall. It was a pretty toy. Nello tried to find its owner, and, failing, thought that it was just the thing to please Alois.

It was quite night when he passed the millhouse: he knew the little window of her room. It could be no harm, he thought, if he gave her his little piece of treasure-trove, they had been playfellows so long. There was a shed with a sloping roof beneath her casement: he climbed it and tapped softly at the lattice: there was a little light within. The child opened it and looked out half frightened.

Nello put the tambourine-player into her hands. "Here is a doll I found in the snow, Alois. Take it," he whispered—"take it, and God bless thee, dear!"

He slid down from the shed roof before she had time to thank him, and ran off through the darkness.

That night there was a fire at the mill. Outbuildings and much corn were destroyed although the mill itself and the dwelling house were unharmed. All the village was out in terror, and engines came tearing through the snow from Antwerp. The miller was insured, and would lose nothing: nevertheless, he was in furious wrath, and declared aloud that the fire was due to no accident, but to some foul intent.

Nello, awakened from his sleep, ran to help with the

"Here is a doll I found in the snow, Alois"

rest: Baas Cogez thrust him angrily aside. "Thou wert loitering here after dark," he said roughly. "I believe that thou dost know more of the fire than any one."

Nello heard him in silence, stupefied, not supposing that any one could say such things except in jest, and not comprehending how any one could pass a jest at such a time.

Nevertheless, the miller said the brutal thing openly to many of his neighbors in the day that followed; and though no serious charge was ever preferred against the lad, it got bruited about that Nello had been seen in the mill yard after dark on some unspoken errand, and that he bore Baas Cogez a grudge for forbidding his intercourse with little Alois; and so the hamlet, which followed the sayings of its richest landowner servilely, and whose families all hoped to secure the riches of Alois in some future time for their sons, took the hint to give grave looks and cold words to old Jehan Daas's grandson. No one said anything to him openly, but all the village agreed together to humor the miller's prejudice, and at the cottages and farms where Nello and Patrasche called every morning for the milk for Antwerp, downcast glances and brief phrases replaced to them the broad smiles and cheerful greetings to which they had been always used. No one really credited the miller's absurd suspicion, nor the outrageous accusations born of them, but the people were all very poor and very ignorant, and the one rich man of the place had pronounced against him. Nello, in his innocence and his friendlessness, had no strength to stem the popular tide.

"Thou art very cruel to the lad," the miller's wife dared to say, weeping, to her lord. "Sure he is an innocent lad and a faithful, and would never dream of any such wickedness, however sore his heart might be."

But Baas Cogez being an obstinate man, having once

said a thing held to it doggedly, though in his innermost soul he knew well the injustice that he was committing.

Meanwhile, Nello endured the injury done against him with a certain proud patience that disdained to complain: he only gave way a little when he was quite alone with old Patrasche. Besides, he thought, "If it should win! They will be sorry then, perhaps."

Still, to a boy not quite sixteen, and who had dwelt in one little world all his short life, and in his childhood had been caressed and applauded on all sides, it was a hard trial to have the whole of that little world turn against him for naught. Especially hard in that bleak, snow-bound, famine-stricken wintertime, when the only light and warmth there could be found abode beside the village hearths and in the kindly greetings of neighbors. In the wintertime all drew nearer to each other, all to all, except to Nello and Patrasche, with whom none now would have anything to do, and who were left to care as they might with the old paralyzed, bedridden man in the little cabin, whose fire was often low, and whose board was often without bread, for there was a buyer from Antwerp who had taken to drive his mule in of a day for the milk of the various dairies, and there were only three or four of the people who had refused his terms of purchase and remained faithful to the little green cart. So that the burden which Patrasche drew had become very light, and the centime pieces in Nello's pouch had become, alas! very small likewise.

The dog would stop, as usual, at all the familiar gates which were now closed to him, and look up at them with wistful, mute appeal; and it cost the neighbors a pang to shut their doors and their hearts, and let Patrasche draw his cart on again, empty. Nevertheless, they did it, for they desired to please Baas Cogez.

Noël was close at hand.

The weather was very wild and cold. The snow was six feet deep, and the ice was firm enough to bear oxen and men upon it everywhere. At this season the little village was always gay and cheerful. At the poorest dwelling there were possets and cakes, joking and dancing, sugared saints and gilded Jésus. The merry Flemish bells jingled everywhere on the horses; everywhere within doors some well-filled soup-pot sang and smoked over the stove; and everywhere over the snow without laughing maidens pattered in bright kerchiefs and stout kirtles, going to and from the mass. Only in the little hut it was very dark and very cold.

Nello and Patrasche were left utterly alone, for one night in the week before the Christmas Day, Death entered there, and took away from life forever old Jehan Daas, who had never known of life aught save its poverty and its pains. He had long been half dead, incapable of any movement except a feeble gesture, and powerless for anything beyond a gentle word; and yet his loss fell on them both with a great horror in it: they mourned him passionately. He had passed away from them in his sleep, and when in the gray dawn they learned their bereavement, unutterable solitude and desolation seemed to close around them. He had long been only a poor, feeble, paralyzed old man, who could not raise a hand in their defense, but he had loved them well: his smile had always welcomed their return. They mourned for him unceasingly, refusing to be comforted, as in the white winter day they followed the deal shell that held his body to the nameless grave by the little gray church. They were his only mourners, these two whom he had left friendless upon earth—the young boy and the old dog.

"Surely, he will relent now and let the poor lad come

hither?" thought the miller's wife, glancing at her husband where he smoked by the hearth.

Baas Cogez knew her thought, but he hardened his heart, and would not unbar his door as the little, humble funeral went by. "The boy is a beggar," he said to himself: "he shall not be about Alois."

The woman dared not say anything aloud, but when the grave was closed and the mourners had gone, she put a wreath of immortelles into Alois's hands and bade her go and lay it reverently on the dark, unmarked mound where the snow was displaced.

Nello and Patrasche went home with broken hearts. But even of that poor, melancholy, cheerless home they were denied the consolation. There was a month's rent overdue for their little home, and when Nello had paid the last sad service to the dead he had not a coin left. He went and begged grace of the owner of the hut, a cobbler who went every Sunday night to drink his pint of wine and smoke with Baas Cogez. The cobbler would grant no mercy. He was a harsh, miserly man, and loved money. He claimed in default of his rent every stick and stone, every pot and pan, in the hut, and bade Nello and Patrasche be out of it on the morrow.

Now, the cabin was lowly enough, and in some sense miserable enough, and yet their hearts clove to it with a great affection. They had been so happy there, and in the summer, with its clambering vine and its flowering beans, it was so pretty and bright in the midst of the sunlighted fields! There life in it had been full of labor and privation, and yet they had been so well content, so gay of heart, running together to meet the old man's never-failing smile of welcome!

All night long the boy and the dog sat by the fireless hearth in the darkness, drawn close together for warmth and sorrow. Their bodies were insensible to the cold, but their hearts seemed frozen in them.

When the morning broke over the white, chill earth it was the morning of Christmas Eve. With a shudder, Nello clasped close to him his only friend, while his tears fell hot and fast on the dog's frank forehead. "Let us go, Patrasche—dear, dear Patrasche," he murmured. "We will not wait to be kicked out: let us go."

Patrasche had no will but his, and they went sadly, side by side, out from the little place which was so dear to them both, and in which every humble, homely thing was to them precious and beloved. Patrasche drooped his head wearily as he passed by his own green cart: it was no longer his—it had to go with the rest to pay the rent, and his brass harness lay idle and glittering on the snow. The dog could have lain down beside it and died for very heartsickness as he went, but whilst the lad lived and needed him Patrasche would not yield and give way.

They took the old accustomed road into Antwerp. The day had yet scarce more than dawned, most of the shutters were still closed, but some of the villagers were about. They took no notice whilst the dog and the boy passed by them. At one door Nello paused and looked wistfully within: his grandfather had done many a kindly turn in neighbor's service to the people who dwelt there.

"Would you give Patrasche a crust?" he said, timidly. "He is old, and he has had nothing since last forenoon."

The woman shut the door hastily, murmuring some vague saying about wheat and rye being very dear that season. The boy and the dog went on again wearily: they asked no more. By slow and painful ways they reached Antwerp as the chimes tolled ten.

"If I had anything about me I could sell to get him

bread!" thought Nello, but he had nothing except the wisp of linen and serge that covered him, and his pair of wooden shoes.

Patrasche understood, and nestled his nose into the lad's hand, as though to pray him not to be disquieted for any woe or want of his.

The winner of the drawing-prize was to be proclaimed at noon, and to the public building where he had left his treasure Nello made his way. On the steps and in the entrance-hall there was a crowd of youths—some of his age, some older, all with parents or relatives or friends. His heart was sick with fear as he went among them, holding Patrasche close to him. The great bells of the city clashed out the hour of noon with brazen clamor. The doors of the inner hall were opened; the eager, panting throng rushed in: it was known that the selected picture would be raised above the rest upon a wooden dais.

A mist obscured Nello's sight, his head swam, his limbs almost failed him. When his vision cleared he saw the drawing raised on high: it was not his own! A slow, sonorous voice was proclaiming aloud that victory had been adjudged to Stephan Kiesslinger, born in the burgh of Antwerp, son of a wharfinger in that town.

When Nello recovered his consciousness he was lying on the stones without, and Patrasche was trying with every art he knew to call him back to life. In the distance a throng of the youths of Antwerp were shouting around their successful comrade, and escorting him with acclamations to his home upon the quay.

The boy staggered to his feet and drew the dog into his embrace. "It is all over, dear Patrasche," he murmured—"all over!"

He rallied himself as best he could, for he was weak

from fasting, and retraced his steps to the village. Patrasche paced by his side with his head drooping and his old limbs feeble from hunger and sorrow.

The snow was falling fast: a keen hurricane blew from the north: it was bitter as death on the plains. It took them long to traverse the familiar path, and the bells were sounding four of the clock as they approached the hamlet. Suddenly Patrasche paused, arrested by a scent in the snow, scratched, whined, and drew out with his teeth a small case of brown leather. He held it up to Nello in the darkness. Where they were there stood a little Calvary, and a lamp burned dully under the cross: the boy mechanically turned the case to the light: on it was the name of Baas Cogez, and within it were notes for two thousand francs.

The sight roused the lad a little from his stupor. He thrust it in his shirt, and stroked Patrasche and drew him onward. The dog looked up wistfully in his face.

Nello made straight for the millhouse, and went to the house door and struck on its panels. The miller's wife opened it weeping, with little Alois clinging close to her skirts. "Is it thee, thou poor lad?" she said kindly through her tears. "Get thee gone ere the Baas see thee. We are in sore trouble to-night. He is out seeking for a power of money that he has let fall riding homeward, and in this snow he never will find it; and God knows it will go nigh to ruin us. It is Heaven's own judgment for the things we have done to thee."

Nello put the note-case in her hand and called Patrasche within the house. "Patrasche found the money to-night," he said quickly. "Tell Baas Cogez so: I think he will not deny the dog shelter and food in his old age. Keep him from pursuing me, and I pray of you to be good to him."

Ere either woman or dog knew what he meant he had stooped and kissed Patrasche: then closed the door hurriedly, and disappeared in the gloom of the fast-falling night.

The woman and the child stood speechless with joy and fear: Patrasche vainly spent the fury of his anguish against the iron-bound oak of the barred house-door. They did not dare unbar the door and let him forth: they tried all they could to solace him. They brought him sweet cakes and juicy meats; they tempted him with the best they had; they tried to lure him to abide by the warmth of the hearth, but to no avail. Patrasche refused to be comforted or to stir from the barred portal.

It was six o'clock when from an opposite entrance the miller at last came, jaded and broken, into his wife's presence. "It is lost forever," he said with an ashen cheek and a quiver in his stern voice. "We have looked with lanterns everywhere: it is gone—the little maiden's portion and all!"

His wife put the money into his hand, and told him how it had come to her. The strong man sank trembling into a seat and covered his face, ashamed and almost afraid. "I have been cruel to the lad," he muttered at length: "I deserved not to have good at his hands."

Little Alois, taking courage, crept close to her father and nestled against him her fair curly head. "Nello may come here again, father?" she whispered. "He may come to-morrow as he used to do?"

The miller pressed her in his arms: his hard, sunburned face was very pale and his mouth trembled. "Surely, surely," he answered his child. "He shall bide here on Christmas Day, and any other day he will. God helping me, I will make amends to the boy—I will make amends."

Little Alois kissed him in gratitude and joy, then slid from his knees and ran to where the dog kept watch by the door. "And to-night I may feast Patrasche?" she cried in a child's thoughtless glee.

Her father bent his head gravely: "Ay, ay: let the dog have the best;" for the stern old man was moved and shaken to his heart's depths.

It was Christmas Eve, and the mill-house was filled with oak logs and squares of turf, with cream and honey, with meat and bread, and the rafters were hung with wreaths of evergreen, and the Calvary and the cuckoo clock looked out from a mass of holly. There were little paper lanterns, too, for Alois, and toys of various fashions and sweetmeats in bright-pictured papers. There were light and warmth and abundance everywhere, and the child would fain have made the dog a guest honored and feasted.

But Patrasche would neither lie in the warmth nor share in the cheer. Famished he was and very cold, but without Nello he would partake neither of comfort nor food. Against all temptation he was proof, and close against the door he leaned always, watching only for a means of escape.

"He wants the lad," said Baas Cogez. "Good dog! good dog! I will go over to the lad the first thing at day-dawn." For no one but Patrasche knew that Nello had left the hut, and no one but Patrasche divined that Nello had gone to face starvation and misery alone.

The mill kitchen was very warm: great logs crackled and flamed on the hearth; neighbors came in for a glass of wine and a slice of the fat goose baking for supper. Alois, gleeful and sure of her playmate back on the morrow, bounded and sang and tossed back her yellow hair. Baas Cogez, in the fullness of his heart, smiled on her through moistened eyes, and spoke of the way in which he would befriend her favorite companion; the housemother sat with calm, contented face at the spinning wheel; the cuckoo in the clock chirped mirthful hours. Amidst it all Patrasche was bidden with a thousand words of welcome to tarry there a cherished guest. But neither peace nor plenty could allure him where Nello was not.

When the supper smoked on the board, and the voices were loudest and gladdest, and the Christ-child brought choicest gifts to Alois, Patrasche, watching always an occasion, glided out when the door was unlatched by a careless newcomer, and as swiftly as his weak and tired limbs would bear him sped over the snow in the bitter, black night. He had only one thought—to follow Nello. A human friend might have paused for the pleasant meal, the cheery warmth, the cosy slumber; but that was not the friendship of Patrasche. He remembered a bygone time, when an old man and a little child had found him sick unto death in the wayside ditch.

Snow had fallen freshly all the evening long; it was now nearly ten; the trail of the boy's footsteps was almost obliterated. It took Patrasche long to discover any scent. When at last he found it, it was lost again quickly, and again lost and again recovered, a hundred times or more.

The night was very wild. The lamps under the wayside crosses were blown out; the roads were sheets of ice; the impenetrable darkness hid every trace of habitations; there was no living thing abroad. All the cattle were housed, and in all the huts and homesteads men and women rejoiced and feasted. There was only Patrasche out in the cruel cold—old and famished and full of pain, but with the strength and the patience of a great love to sustain him in his search.

The trail of Nello's steps, faint and obscure as it was under the new snow, went straightly along the accustomed tracks into Antwerp. It was past midnight when Patrasche traced it over the boundaries of the town and into the narrow, tortuous, gloomy streets. It was all quite dark in the town, save where some light gleamed ruddily through the crevices of house-shutters or some group went homeward with lanterns chanting drinking songs. The streets were all white with ice: the high walls and roofs loomed black against them. There was scarce a sound save the riot of the winds down the passages as they tossed the creaking signs and shook the tall lamp-irons.

So many passers-by had trodden through and through the snow, so many diverse paths had crossed and recrossed each other, that the dog had a hard task to retain any hold on the track he followed. But he kept on his way, though the cold pierced him to the bone, and the jagged ice cut his feet, and the hunger in his body gnawed like a rat's teeth. He kept on his way, a poor gaunt, shivering thing, and by long patience traced the steps he loved into the very heart of the burgh and up to the steps of the great cathedral.

"He is gone to the things that he loved," thought Patrasche: he could not understand, but he was full of sorrow and of pity for the art-passion that to him was so incomprehensible and yet so sacred.

The portals of the cathedral were unclosed after the midnight mass. Some heedlessness in the custodians, too eager to go home and feast or sleep, or too drowsy to know whether they turned the keys aright, had left one of the doors unlocked. By that accident the footfalls Patrasche sought had passed through into the building, leaving the white marks of snow upon the dark stone floor. By that slender white thread, frozen as it fell, he was guided through the intense silence, through the immensity of the vaulted space—guided straight to the gates of the chancel, and, stretched there upon the stones, he found Nello. He crept up and touched the face of the boy. "Didst thou dream that I should be faithless and forsake thee? I—a dog?" said that mute carcass.

The lad raised himself with a low cry and clasped him close. "Let us lie down and die together," he murmured. "Men have no need of us, and we are all alone."

In answer, Patrasche crept closer yet, and laid his head upon the young boy's breast. The great tears stood in his brown, sad eyes: not for himself—for himself he was happy.

They lay close together in the piercing cold. The blasts that blew over the Flemish dikes from the northern seas were like waves of ice, which froze every living thing they touched. The interior of the immense vault of stone in which they were was even more bitterly chill than the snow-covered plains without. Now and then a bat moved in the shadows—now and then a gleam of light came on the ranks of carven figures. Under the Rubens they lay together quite still, and soothed almost into a dreaming slumber by the numbing narcotic of the cold. Together they dreamed of the old glad days when they had chased each other through the flowering grasses of the summer meadows, or sat hidden in the tall bulrushes by the water's side, watching the boats go seaward in the sun.

Suddenly through the darkness a great white radiance streamed through the vastness of the aisles; the moon, that was at her height, had broken through the clouds, the snow had ceased to fall, the light reflected from the snow without was clear as the light of dawn. It fell through the arches full upon the two pictures above, from which the boy on his entrance had flung back the veil: the Elevation

The lad raised himself with a low cry and clasped him close

and the Descent of the Cross were for one instant visible.

Nello rose to his feet and stretched his arms to them; the tears of a passionate ecstasy glistened on the paleness of his face. "I have seen them at last!" he cried aloud. "O God, it is enough!"

His limbs failed under him, and he sank upon his knees, still gazing upward at the majesty that he adored. For a few brief moments the light illumined the divine visions that had been denied to him so long—light clear and sweet and strong as though it streamed from the throne of Heaven. Then suddenly it passed away: once more a great darkness covered the face of Christ.

The arms of the boy drew close again the body of the dog. "We shall see His face—*there*," he murmured; "and He will not part us, I think."

On the morrow, by the chancel of the cathedral, the people of Antwerp found them both. They were both dead: the cold of the night had frozen into stillness alike the young life and the old. When the Christmas morning broke and the priests came to the temple, they saw them lying thus on the stones together. Above, the veils were drawn back from the great visions of Rubens, and the fresh rays of the sunrise touched the thorn-crowned head of the Christ.

As the day grew on there came an old, hard-featured man who wept as women weep. "I was cruel to the lad," he muttered, "and now I would have made amends—yea, to the half of my substance—and he should have been to me as a son."

There came also, as the day grew apace, a painter who had fame in the world, and who was liberal of hand and of spirit. "I seek one who should have had the prize yesterday had worth won," he said to the people—"a boy

of rare promise and genius. An old wood-cutter on a
fallen tree at eventide—that was all his theme. But there
was greatness for the future in it. I would fain find him,
and take him with me and teach him Art."

And a little child with curling fair hair, sobbing bitterly
as she clung to her father's arm, cried aloud, "Oh, Nello,
come! We have all ready for thee. The Christ-child's
hands are full of gifts, and the old piper will play for us;
and the mother says thou shalt stay by the hearth and
burn nuts with us all the Noël week long—yes, even to the
Feast of the Kings! And Patrasche will be so happy!
Oh, Nello, wake and come!"

But the young pale face, turned upward to the light of
the great Rubens with a smile upon its mouth, answered
them all, "It is too late."

For the sweet, sonorous bells went ringing through the
frost, and the sunlight shone upon the plains of snow, and
the populace trooped gay and glad through the streets,
but Nello and Patrasche no more asked charity at their
hands. All they needed now Antwerp gave unbidden.

Death had been more pitiful to them than longer life
would have been. It had taken the one in the loyalty of
love, and the other in the innocence of faith, from a world
which for love has no recompense and for faith no
fulfillment.

All their lives they had been together, and in their
deaths they were not divided: for when they were found
the arms of the boy were folded too closely around the
dog to be severed without violence, and the people of their
little village, contrite and ashamed, implored a special
grace for them, and, making them one grave, laid them to
rest there side by side—forever!

THE NÜRNBERG STOVE

"I shall soon be home with dear Hirschvogel!"

THE NÜRNBERG STOVE

Augustus lived in a little town called Hall. Hall is a
favorite name for several towns in Austria and in Ger-
many; but this one especial little Hall, in the Upper
Innthal, is one of the most charming Old-World places
that I know, and August for his part did not know any
other. It has the green meadows and the great mountains
all about it, and the gray-green glacier-fed water rushes
by it.

It has paved streets and enchanting little shops that
have all latticed panes and iron gratings to them; it has a
very grand old Gothic church that has the noblest
blendings of light and shadow, and marble tombs of dead
knights, and a look of infinite strength and repose as a
church should have.

Then there is the Muntze Tower, black and white,
rising out of greenery and looking down on a long
wooden bridge and the broad rapid river; and there is an
old schloss which has been made into a guardhouse, with

battlements and frescoes and heraldic devices in gold and colors, and a man-at-arms carved in stone standing life-size in his niche and bearing his date 1530.

A little farther on, but close at hand, is a cloister with beautiful marble columns and tombs, and a colossal wood-carved Calvary, and beside that a small and very rich chapel: indeed, so full is the little town of the undisturbed past, that to walk in it is like opening a missal of the Middle Ages, all emblazoned and illuminated with saints and warriors, and it is so clean, and so still, and so noble, by reason of its monuments and its historic color, that I marvel much no one has ever cared to sing its praises. The old pious heroic life of an age at once more restful and more brave than ours still leaves its spirit there, and then there is the girdle of the mountains all around, and that alone means strength, peace, majesty.

In this little town a few years ago August Strehla lived with his people in the stone-paved irregular square where the grand church stands.

He was a small boy of nine years at that time—a chubby-faced little man with rosy cheeks, big hazel eyes, and clusters of curls the brown of ripe nuts. His mother was dead, his father was poor, and there were many mouths at home to feed. In this country the winters are long and very cold, the whole land lies wrapped in snow for many months, and this night that he was trotting home, with a jug of beer in his numb red hands, was terribly cold and dreary. The good burghers of Hall had shut their double shutters, and the few lamps there were flickered dully behind their quaint, old-fashioned iron casings. The mountains indeed were beautiful, all snow-white under the stars that are so big in frost. Hardly anyone was astir; a few good souls wending home from vespers, a tired post-boy who blew a shrill blast from his tasseled horn, as he pulled up his sledge before a hostelry, and little August hugging his jug of beer to his ragged sheepskin coat, were all who were abroad, for the snow fell heavily and the good folks of Hall go early to their beds. He could not run, or he would have spilled the beer; he was half frozen and a little frightened, but he kept up his courage by saying over and over again to himself, "I shall soon be at home with dear Hirschvogel."

He went on through the streets, past the stone man-at-arms of the guardhouse, and so into the place where the great church was, and where near it stood his father Karl Strehla's house, with a sculptured Bethlehem over the doorway, and the Pilgrimage of the Three Kings painted on its wall. He had been sent on a long errand outside the gates in the afternoon, over the frozen fields and the broad white snow, and had been belated, and had thought he had heard the wolves behind him at every step, and had reached the town in a great state of terror, thankful with all his little panting heart to see the oil-lamp burning under the first house-shrine. But he had not forgotten to call for the beer, and he carried it carefully now, though his hands were so numb that he was afraid they would let the jug down every moment.

The snow outlined with white every gable and cornice of the beautiful old wooden houses; the moonlight shone on the gilded signs, the lambs, the grapes, the eagles, and all the quaint devices that hung before the doors; covered lamps burned before the Nativities and Crucifixions painted on the walls or let into the woodwork; here and there, where a shutter had not been closed, a ruddy firelight lit up a homely interior, with the noisy band of children clustering round the housemother and a big brown loaf, or some gossips spinning and listening to the cobbler's or the barber's story of a neighbor, while the oil wicks glimmered, and the hearthlogs blazed, and the chestnuts sputtered in their iron roasting-pot.

Little August saw all these things as he saw everything with his two big bright eyes that had such curious lights and shadows in them; but he went heedfully on his way for the sake of the beer which a single slip of the foot would make him spill.

At his knock and call the solid oak door, four centuries old if one, flew open, and the boy darted in with his beer, and shouted, with all the force of mirthful lungs, "Oh, dear Hirschvogel, but for the thought of you I should have died!"

It was a large barren room into which he rushed with so much pleasure, and the bricks were bare and uneven. It had a walnut-wood press, handsome and very old, a broad deal table, and several wooden stools for all its furniture; but at the top of the chamber, sending out warmth and color together as the lamp shed its rays upon it, was a tower of porcelain, burnished with all the hues of a king's peacock and a queen's jewels, and surmounted with armed figures, and shields, and flowers of heraldry, and a great golden crown upon the highest summit of all.

It was a stove of 1532, and on it were the letters H. R. H., for it was in every portion the handiwork of the great potter of Nürnberg, Augustin Hirschvogel, who put his mark thus, as all the world knows.

The stove no doubt had stood in palaces and been made for princes, had warmed the crimson stockings of cardinals and the gold-broidered shoes of archduchesses, had glowed in presence-chambers and lent its carbon to help kindle sharp brains in anxious councils of state; no one knew what it had seen or done or been fashioned for: but it was a right royal thing. Yet perhaps it had never been more useful than it was now in this poor desolate room, sending down heat and comfort into the troop of children tumbled together on a wolf-skin at its feet, who received frozen August among them with loud shouts of joy.

"Oh, dear Hirschvogel, I am so cold, so cold!" said August, kissing its gilded lion's claws. "Is father not in, Dorothea?"

"No, dear. He is late."

Dorothea was a girl of seventeen, dark-haired and serious, and with a sweet sad face, for she had had many cares laid on her shoulders, even whilst still a mere baby. She was the eldest of the Strehla family; and there were ten of them in all.

Next to her there came Jan and Karl and Otho, big lads, gaining a little for their own living; and then came August, who went up in the summer to the high alps with the farmers' cattle, but in winter could do nothing to fill his own little platter and pot; and then all the little ones, who could only open their mouths to be fed like young birds,—Albrecht and Hilda, and Waldo and Christof, and last of all little three-year-old Ermengilda, with eyes like forget-me-nots, whose birth had cost them the life of their mother.

They were of that mixed race, half Austrian, half Italian, so common in the Tyrol; some of the children were white and golden as lilies, others were brown and brilliant as fresh-fallen chestnuts.

The father was a good man, but weak and weary with so many to find for and so little to do it with. He worked at the salt furnaces, and by that gained a few florins; people said he would have worked better and kept his family more easily if he had not loved his pipe and a draft of ale too well; but this had only been said of him after his wife's death, when trouble and perplexity had begun to dull a brain never too vigorous, and to enfeeble further a character already too yielding. As it was, the wolf often bayed at the door of the Strehla household, without a wolf from the mountains coming down.

Dorothea was one of those maidens who almost work miracles, so far can their industry and care and intelligence make a home sweet and wholesome and a single loaf seem to swell into twenty. The children were always clean and happy, and the table was seldom without its big pot of soup once a day. Still, very poor they were, and Dorothea's heart ached with shame, for she knew that their father's debts were many for flour and meat and clothing.

Of fuel to feed the big stove they had always enough without cost, for their mother's father was alive, and sold wood and fir cones and coke, and never grudged them to his grandchildren, though he grumbled at Strehla's improvidence and hapless, dreamy ways.

"Father says we are never to wait for him: we will have supper, now you have come home, dear," said Dorothea, who, however she might fret her soul in secret as she knitted their hose and mended their shirts, never let her anxieties cast a gloom on the children; only to August she did speak a little sometimes, because he was so thoughtful and so tender of her always, and knew as well as she did that there were troubles about money—though these troubles were vague to them both, and the debtors were patient and kindly, being neighbors all in the old twisting streets between the guardhouse and the river.

Supper was a huge bowl of soup, with big slices of brown bread swimming in it and some onions bobbing up and down: the bowl was soon emptied by ten wooden spoons, and then the three eldest boys slipped off to bed, being tired with their rough bodily labor in the snow all day, and Dorothea drew her spinning wheel by the stove and set it whirring, and the little ones got August down upon the old worn wolf-skin and clamored to him for a picture or a story. For August was the artist of the family.

He had a piece of planed deal that his father had given him, and some sticks of charcoal, and he would draw a hundred things he had seen in the day, sweeping each out with his elbow when the children had seen enough of it and sketching another in its stead—faces and dogs' heads, and men in sledges, and old women in their furs, and pine trees, and cocks and hens, and all sorts of animals, and now and then—very reverently—a Madonna and Child. It was all very rough, for there was no one to teach him anything. But it was all lifelike, and kept the whole troop of children shrieking with laughter, or watching breathless, with wide-open, wondering, awed eyes.

They were all so happy: what did they care for the snow outside? Their little bodies were warm, and their hearts merry; even Dorothea, troubled about the bread for the morrow, laughed as she spun; and August, with all his soul in his work, and little rosy Ermengilda's cheek on his shoulder, glowing after his frozen afternoon, cried out loud, smiling, as he looked up at the stove that was shedding its heat down on them all—

"Oh, dear Hirschvogel! you are almost as great and good as the sun! No, you are greater and better, I think, because he goes away nobody knows where all these long, dark, cold hours, and does not care how people die for want of him; but you—you are always ready: just a little bit of wood to feed you, and you will make a summer for us all the winter through!"

The grand old stove seemed to smile through all its

iridescent surface at the praises of the child. No doubt the stove, though it had known three centuries and more, had known but very little gratitude.

It was one of those magnificent stoves in enameled faïence which so excited the jealousy of the other potters of Nürnberg that in a body they demanded of the magistracy that Augustin Hirschvogel should be forbidden to make any more of them—the magistracy, happily, proving of a broader mind, and having no sympathy with the wish of the artisans to cripple their greater fellow.

It was of great height and breadth, with all the majolica luster which Hirschvogel learned to give to his enamels when he was making love to the young Venetian girl whom he afterwards married. There was the statue of a king at each corner, modeled with as much force and splendor as his friend Albrecht Dürer could have given unto them on copperplate or canvas. The body of the stove itself was divided into panels, which had the Ages of Man painted on them in polychrome; the borders of the panels had roses and holly and laurel and other foliage, and German mottoes in black letter of odd Old-World moralizing, such as the old Teutons, and the Dutch after them, love to have on their chimneyplaces and their drinking cups, their dishes and flagons. The whole was burnished with gilding in many parts, and was radiant everywhere with that brilliant coloring of which the Hirschvogel family, painters on glass and great in chemistry as they were, were all masters.

The stove was a very grand thing, as I say: possibly Hirschvogel had made it for some mighty lord of the Tyrol at that time when he was an imperial guest at Innspruck and fashioned so many things for the Schloss Amras and beautiful Philippine Welser, the burgher's daughter, who gained an archduke's heart by her beauty and the right to wear his honors by her wit. Nothing was known of the stove at this latter day in Hall. The grandfather Strehla, who had been a mastermason, had dug it up out of some ruins where he was building, and, finding it without a flaw, had taken it home, and only thought it worth finding because it was such a good one to burn. That was now sixty years past, and ever since then the stove had stood in the big desolate empty room, warming three generations of the Strehla family, and having seen nothing prettier perhaps in all its many years than the children tumbled now in a cluster like gathered flowers at its feet. For the Strehla children, born to nothing else, were all born with beauty: white or brown, they were equally lovely to look upon, and when they went into the church to mass, with their curling locks and their clasped hands, they stood under the grim statues like cherubs flown down off some fresco.

"Tell us a story, August," they cried, in chorus, when they had seen charcoal pictures till they were tired; and August did as he did every night, pretty nearly—looked up at the stove and told them what he imagined of the many adventures and joys and sorrows of the human being who figured on the panels from his cradle to his grave.

To the children the stove was a household god. In summer they laid a mat of fresh moss all round it, and dressed it up with green boughs and the numberless beautiful wild flowers of the Tyrol country. In winter all their joys centered in it, and scampering home from school over the ice and snow they were happy, knowing that they would soon be cracking nuts or roasting chestnuts in the broad ardent glow of its noble tower, which rose eight feet high above them with all its spires and pinnacles and crowns.

Once a traveling peddler had told them that the letters on it meant Augustin Hirschvogel, and that Hirschvogel had been a great German potter and painter, like his father before him, in the art-sanctified city of Nürnberg, and had made many such stoves, that were all miracles of beauty and of workmanship, putting all his heart and his soul and his faith into his labors, as the men of those earlier ages did, and thinking but little of gold or praise.

An old trader too, who sold curiosities not far from the church, had told August a little more about the brave family of Hirschvogel, whose houses can be seen in Nürnberg to this day; of old Veit, the first of them, who painted the Gothic windows of St. Sebald with the marriage of the Margravine; of his sons and of his grandsons, potters, painters, engravers all, and chief of them great Augustin, the Luca della Robbia of the North. And August's imagination, always quick, had made a living personage out of these few records, and saw Hirschvogel as though he were in the flesh walking up and down the Maximilian-Strass in his visit to Innspruck, and maturing beautiful things in his brain as he stood on the bridge and gazed on the emerald-green flood of the Inn.

So the stove had got to be called Hirschvogel in the family, as if it were a living creature, and little August was very proud because he had been named after that famous old dead German who had had the genius to make so glorious a thing. All the children loved the stove, but with August the love of it was a passion; and in his secret heart he used to say to himself, "When I am a man, I will make just such things too, and then I will set Hirschvogel in a beautiful room in a house that I will build myself in Innspruck just outside the gates, where the chestnuts are, by the river: that is what I will do when I am a man."

For August, a salt-baker's son, and a little cowkeeper when he was anything, was a dreamer of dreams, and when he was upon the high alps with his cattle, with the stillness and the sky around him, was quite certain that he would live for greater things than driving the herds up when the spring-tide came among the blue sea of gentians, or toiling down in the town with wood and with timber as his father and grandfather did every day of their lives. He was a strong and healthy little fellow, fed on the free mountain air, and he was very happy, and loved his family devotedly, and was as active as a squirrel and as playful as a hare; but he kept his thoughts to himself, and some of them went a very long way for a little boy who was only one among many, and to whom nobody had ever paid any attention except to teach him his letters and tell him to fear God. August in winter was only a little hungry schoolboy, trotting to be catechised by the priest, or to bring the loaves from the bakehouse, or to carry his father's boots to the cobbler; and in summer he was only one of hundreds of cowboys, who drove the poor, half-blind, blinking, stumbling cattle, ringing their throat-bells, out into the sweet intoxication of the sudden sunlight, and lived up with them in the heights among the Alpine roses, with only the clouds and the snow summits near. But he was always thinking, thinking, thinking, for all that; and under his little sheepskin winter coat and his rough hempen summer shirt, his heart had as much courage in it as Hofer's ever had—great Hofer, who is a household word in all the Innthal, and whom August always reverently remembered when he went to the city of Innspruck and ran out by the foaming watermill and under the wooded height of Berg Isel.

August lay now in the warmth of the stove and told the children stories, his own little brown face growing red with excitement as his imagination glowed to fever heat. That human being on the panels, who was drawn there as a baby in a cradle, as a boy playing among flowers, as a lover sighing under a casement, as a soldier in the midst of strife, as a father with children round him, as a weary, old, blind man on crutches, and, lastly, as a ransomed soul raised up by angels, had always had the most intense interest for August, and he had made, not one history for him, but a thousand; he seldom told them the same tale twice. He had never seen a storybook in his life; his primer and his massbook were all the volumes he had. But nature had given him Fancy, and she is a good fairy that makes up for the want of very many things! Only, alas! her wings are so very soon broken, poor thing, and then she is of no use at all.

"It is time for you all to go to bed, children," said Dorothea, looking up from her spinning. "Father is very late tonight. You must not sit up for him."

"Oh, five minutes more, dear Dorothea!" they pleaded, and little rosy and golden Ermengilda climbed up into her lap. "Hirschvogel is so warm, the beds are never so warm as he. Cannot you tell us another tale, August?"

"No," cried August, whose face had lost its light, now that his story had come to an end, and who sat serious, with his hands clasped on his knees, gazing onto the luminous arabesques of the stove.

"It is only a week to Christmas," he said suddenly.

"Grandmother's big cakes!" chuckled little Christof, who was five years old, and thought Christmas meant a big cake and nothing else.

"What will Santa Claus find for 'Gilda if she be good?" murmured Dorothea over the child's sunny head; for, however hard poverty might pinch, it could never pinch so tightly that Dorothea would not find some wooden toy and some rosy apples to put in her little sister's socks.

"Father Max has promised me a big goose, because I saved the calf's life in June," said August. It was the twentieth time he had told them so that month, he was so proud of it.

"And Aunt Maïla will be sure to send us wine and honey and a barrel of flour; she always does," said Albrecht. Their aunt Maïla had a châlet and a little farm over on the green slopes towards Dorp Ampas.

"I shall go up into the woods and get Hirschvogel's crown," said August; they always crowned Hirschvogel for Christmas with pine boughs and ivy and mountain berries. The heat soon withered the crown; but it was part of the religion of the day to them, as much so as it was to cross themselves in church and raise their voices in the "O Salutaris Hostia."

And they fell chatting of all they would do on the Christ-night, and one little voice piped loud against another's, and they were as happy as though their stockings would be full of golden purses and jeweled toys, and the big goose in the soup pot seemed to them such a meal as kings would envy.

In the midst of their chatter and laughter a blast of frozen air and a spray of driven snow struck like ice through the room, and reached them even in the warmth of the old wolf skins and the great stove. It was the door which had opened and let in the cold; it was their father who had come home.

The younger children ran joyous to meet him. Dorothea pushed the one wooden armchair of the room to the stove, and August flew to set the jug of beer on a little round table, and fill a long clay pipe; for their father was good to them all, and seldom raised his voice in anger, and they had been trained by the mother they had loved to dutifulness and obedience and a watchful affection.

Tonight Karl Strehla responded very wearily to the young ones' welcome, and came to the wooden chair with a tired step and sat down heavily, not noticing either pipe or beer.

"Are you not well, dear father?" his daughter asked.

"I am well enough," he answered dully, and sat there with his head bent, letting the lighted pipe grow cold.

He was a fair, tall man, gray before his time, and bowed with labor.

"Take the children to bed," he said suddenly, at last, and Dorothea obeyed. August stayed behind, curled before the stove; at nine years old, and when one earns money in the summer from the farmers, one is not altogether a child any more, at least in one's own estimation.

August did not heed his father's silence: he was used to it. Karl Strehla was a man of few words, and, being of weakly health, was usually too tired at the end of the day to do more than drink his beer and sleep. August lay on the wolf skin, dreamy and comfortable, looking up through his drooping eyelids at the golden coronets on the crest of the great stove, and wondering for the millionth time whom it had been made for, and what grand places and scenes it had known.

Dorothea came down from putting the little ones in their beds; the cuckoo clock in the corner struck eight; she looked to her father and the untouched pipe, then sat down to her spinning, saying nothing. She thought he had been drinking in some tavern; it had been often so with him of late.

There was a long silence; the cuckoo called the quarter twice; August dropped asleep, his curls falling over his face; Dorothea's wheel hummed like a cat.

Suddenly Karl Strehla struck his hand on the table, sending the pipe on the ground.

"I have sold Hirschvogel," he said, and his voice was husky and ashamed in his throat. The spinning wheel stopped. August sprang erect out of his sleep.

"Sold Hirschvogel!" If their father had dashed the holy crucifix on the floor at their feet and spat on it, they could not have shuddered under the horror of a greater blasphemy.

"I have sold Hirschvogel!" said Karl Strehla, in the same husky, dogged voice. "I have sold it to a traveling truder in such things for two hundred florins. What would you?—I owe double that. He saw it this morning when you were all out. He will pack it and take it to Munich tomorrow."

Dorothea gave a low shrill cry:

"Oh, father!—the children—in midwinter!"

She turned white as the snow without; her words died away in her throat.

August stood, half blind with sleep, staring with dazed eyes as his cattle stared at the sun when they came out from their winter's prison.

"It is not true! It is not true!" he muttered. "You are jesting, father?"

Strehla broke into a dreary laugh.

"It is true. Would you like to know what is true, too?—that the bread you eat, and the meat you put in this pot, and the roof you have over your heads, are none of them paid for, have been none of them paid for for months and months: if it had not been for your grandfather I should have been in prison all summer and autumn, and he is out of patience and will do no more now. There is no work to be had; the masters go to younger men: they say I work ill; it may be so. Who can keep his head above water with ten hungry children dragging him down? When your mother lived, it was different. Boy, you stare at me as if I were a mad dog! You have made a god of yon china thing. Well—it goes: goes tomorrow. Two hundred florins, that is something. It will keep me out of prison for a little, and with the spring things may turn——"

August stood like a creature paralyzed. His eyes were wide open, fastened on his father's with terror and incredulous horror; his face had grown as white as his sister's; his chest heaved with tearless sobs.

"It is not true! It is not true!" he echoed stupidly. It seemed to him that the very skies must fall, and the earth perish, if they could take away Hirschvogel. They might as soon talk of tearing down God's sun out of the heavens.

"You will find it true," said his father doggedly, and angered because he was in his own soul bitterly ashamed to have bartered away the heirloom and treasure of his race and the comfort and health-giver of his young children. "You will find it true. The dealer has paid me half the money tonight, and will pay me the other half tomorrow when he packs it up and takes it away to Munich. No doubt it is worth a great deal more—at least I suppose so, as he gives that—but beggars cannot be choosers. The little black stove in the kitchen will warm you all just as well. Who would keep a gilded, painted thing in a poor house like this, when one can make two hundred florins by it? Dorothea, you never sobbed more when your mother died. What is it, when all is said?—a bit of hardware much too grand looking for such a room as this. If all the Strehlas had not been born fools it would have been sold a century ago, when it was dug up out of the ground. 'It is a stove for a museum,' the trader said when he saw it. 'To a museum let it go.'"

August gave a shrill shriek like a hare's when it is caught for its death, and threw himself on his knees at his father's feet.

"Oh, father, father!" he cried, convulsively, his hands closing on Strehla's knees, and his uplifted face blanched and distorted with terror. "Oh, father, dear father, you cannot mean what you say? Send *it* away—our life, our sun, our joy, our comfort? We shall all die in the dark and the cold. Sell *me* rather. Sell me to any trade or any pain you like; I will not mind. But Hirschvogel!—it is like selling the very cross off the altar! You must be in jest. You could not do such a thing—you could not!— you have always been gentle and good, and who have sat in the warmth here year after year with our mother. It is not a piece of hardware, as you say; it is a living thing, for a great man's thoughts and fancies have put life into it, and it loves us though we are only poor little children, and we love it with all our hearts and souls, and up in heaven I am sure the dead Hirschvogel knows! Oh, listen; I will go and try and get work tomorrow! I will ask them to let me cut ice or make the paths through the snow. There must be something I could do, and I will beg the people we owe money to to wait; they are all neighbors, they will be patient. But sell Hirschvogel!—oh, never! never! never! Give the florins back to the vile man. Tell him it would be like selling the shroud out of mother's coffin, or the golden curls off Ermengilda's head! Oh, father, dear father! do hear me, for pity's sake!"

Strehla was moved by the boy's anguish. He loved his children, though he was often weary of them, and their pain was pain to him. But besides emotion, and stronger than emotion, was the anger that August roused in him: he hated and despised himself for the barter of the heirloom of his race, and every word of the child stung him with a stinging sense of shame.

And he spoke in his wrath rather than in his sorrow.

"You are a little fool," he said harshly, as they had never heard him speak. "You rave like a play-actor. Get up and go to bed. The stove is sold. There is no more to be said. Children like you have nothing to do with such matters. The stove is sold, and goes to Munich tomorrow. What is it to you? Be thankful I can get bread for you. Get on your legs, I say, and go to bed."

Strehla took up the jug of ale as he paused, and drained it slowly as a man who had no cares.

August sprang to his feet and threw his hair back off his face; the blood rushed into his cheeks, making them scarlet; his great soft eyes flamed alight with furious passion.

"You *dare* not!" he cried aloud, "you dare not sell it, I say; It is not yours alone; it is ours——"

Strehla flung the emptied jug on the bricks with a force that shivered it to atoms, and, rising to his feet, struck his son a blow that felled him to the floor. It was the first time in all his life that he had ever raised his hand against any one of his children.

Then he took the oil lamp that stood at his elbow and stumbled off to his own chamber with a cloud before his eyes.

"What has happened?" said August, a little while later, as he opened his eyes and saw Dorothea weeping above him on the wolf skin before the stove. He had been struck backward, his head had fallen on the hard bricks where the wolf skin did not reach. He sat up a moment, with his face bent upon his hands.

"I remember now," he said, very low, under his breath.

Dorothea showered kisses on him, while her tears fell like rain.

"But, oh, dear, how could you speak so to father?" she murmured. "It was very wrong."

"No, I was right," said August, and his little mouth, that hitherto had only curled in laughter, curved downward with a fixed and bitter seriousness. "How dare he? How dare he?" he muttered, with his head sunk in his hands. "It is not his alone. It belongs to us all. It is as much yours and mine as it is his."

Dorothea could only sob in answer. She was too frightened to speak. The authority of their parents in the house had never in her remembrance been questioned.

"Are you hurt by the fall, dear August?" she murmured, at length, for he looked to her so pale and strange.

"Yes—no. I do not know. What does it matter?"

He sat up upon the wolf skin with passionate pain upon his face; all his soul was in rebellion, and he was only a child and was powerless.

"It is a sin; it is a theft; it is an infamy," he said slowly, his eyes fastened on the gilded feet of Hirschvogel.

"Oh, August, do not say such things of father!" sobbed his sister. "Whatever he does, *we* ought to think it right."

August laughed aloud.

"Is it right that he should spend his money in drink?—that he should let orders lie unexecuted?—that he should do his work so ill that no one cares to employ him?—that he should live on Grandfather's charity, and then dare sell a thing that is ours every whit as much as it is his? To sell

Hirschvogel! Oh, dear God! I would sooner sell my soul!"

"August!" cried Dorothea, with piteous entreaty. He terrified her, she could not recognize her little, gay, gentle brother in those fierce and blasphemous words.

August laughed aloud again; then all at once his laughter broke down into bitterest weeping. He threw himself forward on the stove, covering it with kisses, and sobbing as though his heart would burst from his bosom.

What could he do? Nothing, nothing, nothing!

"August, dear August," whispred Dorothea, piteously, and trembling all over—for she was a very gentle girl, and fierce feeling terrified her—"August, do not lie there. Come to bed: it is quite late. In the morning you will be calmer. It is horrible indeed, and we shall die of cold, at least the little ones; but if it be father's will——"

"Let me alone," said August, through his teeth, striving to still the storm of sobs that shook him from head to foot. "Let me alone. In the morning!—how can you speak of the morning?"

"Come to bed, dear," sighed his sister. "Oh, August, do not lie and look like that! you frighten me. Do come to bed."

"I shall stay here."

"Here! all night!"

"They might take it in the night. Besides, to leave it *now!*"

"But it is cold! the fire is out."

"It will never be warm any more, nor shall we."

All his childhood had gone out of him, all his gleeful, careless, sunny temper had gone with it; he spoke sullenly and wearily, choking down the great sobs in his chest. To him it was as if the end of the world had come.

His sister lingered by him while striving to persuade

him to his place in the little crowded bedchamber with Albrecht and Waldo and Christof. But it was in vain. "I shall stay here," was all he answered her. And he stayed—all the night long.

The lamps went out; the rats came and ran across the floor; as the hours crept on through midnight and past, the cold intensified and the air of the room grew like ice. August did not move; he lay with his face downward on the golden and rainbow-hued pedestal of the household treasure, which henceforth was to be cold for evermore, an exiled thing in a foreign city in a far-off land.

While yet it was dark his three elder brothers came down the stairs and let themselves out, each bearing his lantern and going to his work in stoneyard and timber yard and at the salt works. They did not notice him; they did not know what had happened.

A little later his sister came down with a light in her hand to make ready the house ere morning should break.

She stole up to him and laid her hand on his shoulder timidly.

"Dear August, you must be frozen. August, do look up! do speak!"

August raised his eyes with a wild, feverish, sullen look in them that she had never seen there. His face was ashen white: his lips were like fire. He had not slept all night; but his passionate sobs had given way to delirious waking dreams and numb senseless trances, which had alternated one on another all through the freezing, lonely, horrible hours.

"It will never be warm again," he muttered, "never again!"

Dorothea clasped him with trembling hands.

"August! do you not know me?" she cried, in an agony.

"I am Dorothea. Wake up, dear—wake up! It is morning, only so dark!"

August shuddered all over.

"The morning!" he echoed.

He slowly rose up onto his feet.

"I will go to Grandfather," he said, very low. "He is always good: perhaps he could save it."

Loud blows with the heavy iron knocker of the house door drowned his words. A strange voice called aloud through the keyhole—

"Let me in! Quick!—there is no time to lose! More snow like this, and the roads will all be blocked. Let me in! Do you hear? I am come to take the great stove."

August sprang erect, his fists doubled, his eyes blazing.

"You shall never touch it!" he screamed, "you shall never touch it!"

"Who shall prevent us?" laughed a big man, who was a Bavarian, amused at the fierce little figure fronting him.

"I!" said August. "You shall never have it! You shall kill me first!"

"Strehla," said the big man, as August's father entered the room, "you have got a little mad dog here: muzzle him."

One way and another they did muzzle him. He fought like a little demon, and hit out right and left, and one of his blows gave the Bavarian a black eye. But he was soon mastered by four grown men, and his father flung him with no light hand out from the door of the back entrance, and the buyers of the stately and beautiful stove set to work to pack it heedfully and carry it away.

When Dorothea stole out to look for August, he was

nowhere in sight. She went back to little 'Gilda, who was ailing, and sobbed over the child, while the others stood looking on, dimly understanding that with Hirschvogel was going all the warmth of their bodies, all the light of their hearth.

Even their father now was sorry and ashamed; but two hundred florins seemed a big sum to him, and, after all, he thought the children could warm themselves quite as well at the black iron stove in the kitchen. Besides, whether he regretted it now or not, the work of the Nürnberg potter was sold irrevocably, and he had to stand still and see the men from Munich wrap it in manifold wrappings and bear it out into the snowy air to where an ox-cart stood in waiting for it.

In another moment Hirschvogel was gone—gone forever and aye.

August had stood still for a time, leaning, sick and faint from the violence that had been used to him, against the back wall of the house. The wall looked on a court where a well was, and the backs of other houses, and beyond them the spire of the Muntze Tower and the peaks of the mountains.

Into the court an old neighbor hobbled for water, and, seeing the boy, said to him—

"Child, is it true your father is selling the big painted stove?"

August nodded, then burst into a passion of tears.

"Well, for sure he is a fool," said the neighbor. "Heaven forgive me for calling him so before his own child! But the stove was worth a mint of money. I do remember in my young days, in old Anton's time (that was your great-grandfather, my lad), a stranger from Vienna saw it, and said it was worth its weight in gold."

August's sobs went on their broken, impetuous course. "I loved it! I loved it!" he moaned. "I do not care what its value was. I loved it. *I loved it!*"

"You little simpleton!" said the old man kindly. "But you are wiser than your father, when all's said. If sell it he must, he should have taken it to good Herr Steiner over at Sprüz, who would have given him honest value. But no doubt they took him over his beer—ay, ay! but if I were you I would do better than cry. I would go after it."

August raised his head, the tears raining down his cheeks.

"Go after it when you are bigger," said the neighbor, with a good-natured wish to cheer him up a little. "The world is a small thing after all: I was a traveling clockmaker once upon a time, and I know that your stove will be safe enough whoever gets it; anything that can be sold for a round sum is always wrapped up in cotton wool by everybody. Ay, ay, don't cry so much; you will see your stove again some day."

Then the old man hobbled away to draw his brazen pail full of water at the well.

August remained leaning against the wall; his head was buzzing and his heart fluttering with the new idea which had presented itself to his mind. "Go after it," the old man had said. He thought, "Why not go with it?" He loved it better than anyone, even better than Dorothea; and he shrank from the thought of meeting his father again, his father who had sold Hirschvogel.

He was by this time in that state of exaltation in which the impossible looks quite natural and commonplace. His tears were still wet on his pale cheeks, but they had ceased to fall. He ran out of the courtyard by a little gate, and across to the huge Gothic porch of the church.

From there he could watch unseen his father's house door, at which were always hanging some blue-and-gray pitchers, such as are common and so picturesque in Austria, for a part of the house was let to a man who dealt in pottery.

He hid himself in the grand portico, which he had so often passed through to go to mass or complin within, and presently his heart gave a great leap, for he saw the straw-enwrapped stove brought out and laid with infinite care on the bullock-dray. Two of the Bavarian men mounted beside it, and the sleigh-wagon slowly crept over the snow of the place—snow crisp and hard as stone. The noble old minster looked its grandest and most solemn, with its dark-gray stone and its vast archways, and its porch that was itself as big as many a church, and its strange gargoyles and lamp-irons black against the snow on its roof and on the pavement; but for once August had no eyes for it: he only watched for his old friend. Then he, a little unnoticeable figure enough, like a score of other boys in Hall, crept, unseen by any of his brothers or sisters, out of the porch and over the shelving uneven square, and followed in the wake of the dray.

Its course lay towards the station of the railway, which is close to the salt-works, whose smoke at times sullies this part of clean little Hall, though it does not do very much damage. From Hall the iron road runs northward through glorious country to Salzburg, Vienna, Prague, Buda, and southward over the Brenner into Italy. Was Hirschvogel going north or south? This at least he would soon know.

August had often hung about the little station, watching the trains come and go and dive into the heart of the hills and vanish. No one said anything to him for idling about; people are kindhearted and easy of temper in this pleasant land, and children and dogs are both happy there. He heard the Bavarians arguing and vociferating a great deal, and learned that they meant to go too and wanted to go with the great stove itself. But this they could not do, for neither could the stove go by passenger train nor they themselves go in a goods train. So at length they insured their precious burden for a large sum, and consented to send it by a luggage train which was to pass through Hall in half an hour. The swift trains seldom deign to notice the existence of Hall at all.

August heard, and a desperate resolve made itself up in his little mind. Where Hirschvogel went would he go. He gave one terrible thought to Dorothea—poor, gentle Dorothea—sitting in the cold at home, then set to work to execute his project. How he managed it he never knew very clearly himself, but certain it is that when the goods train from the north, that had come all the way from Linz on the Danube, moved out of Hall, August was hidden behind the stove in the great covered truck, and wedged, unseen and undreamt of by any human creature, amidst the cases of wood carving, of clocks and clockwork, of Vienna toys, of Turkish carpets, of Russian skins, of Hungarian wines, which shared the same abode as did his swathed and bound Hirschvogel. No doubt he was very naughty, but it never occurred to him that he was so: his whole mind and soul were absorbed in the one entrancing idea, to follow his beloved friend and fire-king.

It was very dark in the closed truck, which had only a little window above the door; and it was crowded, and had a strong smell in it from the Russian hides and the hams that were in it. But August was not frightened; he was close to Hirschvogel, and presently he meant to be closer still; for he meant to do nothing less than get inside Hirschvogel itself. Being a shrewd little boy, and having had by great luck two silver groschen in his breeches-pocket, which he had earned the day before by chopping wood, he had bought some bread and sausage at the station of a woman there who knew him, and who thought he was going out to his uncle Joachim's châlet above Jenbach. This he had with him, and this he ate in the darkness and the lumbering, pounding, thundering noise which made him giddy, as never had he been in a train of any kind before. Still he ate, having had no breakfast, and being a child, and half a German, and not knowing at all how or when he ever would eat again.

When he had eaten, not as much as he wanted, but as much as he thought was prudent (for who could say when he would be able to buy anything more?), he set to work like a little mouse to make a hole in the withes of straw and hay which enveloped the stove. If it had been put in a packing case he would have been defeated at the onset. As it was, he gnawed, and nibbled, and pulled, and pushed, just as a mouse would have done, making his hole where he guessed that the opening of the stove was—the opening through which he had so often thrust the big oak logs to feed it. No one disturbed him; the heavy train went lumbering on and on, and he saw nothing at all of the beautiful mountains, and shining waters, and great forests through which he was being carried. He was hard at work getting through the straw and hay and twisted ropes; and get through them at last he did, and found the door of the stove, which he knew so well, and which was quite large enough for a child of his age to slip through, and it was this which he had counted upon doing.

Slip through he did, as he had often done at home for fun, and curled himself up to see if he could remain there during many hours. He found that he could; air came in through the brass fretwork of the stove; and with admirable caution in such a little fellow he leaned out, drew the hay and straw together, and rearranged the ropes, so that no one could ever have dreamed a little mouse had been at them. Then he curled himself up again, this time more like a dormouse than anything else; and, being safe inside his dear Hirschvogel and intensely cold, he went fast asleep as if he were in his own bed at home with Albrecht and Christof on either side of him. The train lumbered on, stopping often and long, as the habit of goods trains is, sweeping the snow away with its cowswitcher, and rumbling through the deep heart of the mountains, with its lamps aglow like the eyes of a dog in a night of frost.

The train rolled on in its heavy, slow fashion, and the child slept soundly for a long while. When he did awake, it was quite dark outside in the land; he could not see, and of course he was in absolute darkness; and for a while he was sorely frightened, and trembled terribly, and sobbed in a quiet, heartbroken fashion, thinking of them all at home. Poor Dorothea! How anxious she would be! How she would run over the town and walk up to Grandfather's at Dorf Ampas, and perhaps even send over to Jenbach, thinking he had taken refuge with Uncle Joachim! His conscience smote him for the sorrow he must be even then causing to his gentle sister; but it never occurred to him to try and go back. If he once were to lose sight of Hirschvogel how could he ever hope to find it again? How could he ever know whither it had gone— north, south, east, or west? The old neighbor had said that the world was small; but August knew at least that it must have a great many places in it: that he had seen himself on the maps on his schoolhouse walls. Almost any other little boy would, I think, have been frightened out of his wits at the position in which he found himself;

but August was brave, and he had a firm belief that God and Hirschvogel would take care of him. The master potter of Nürnberg was always present to his mind, a kindly, benign, and gracious spirit, dwelling manifestly in that porcelain tower whereof he had been the maker.

A droll fancy, you say? But every child with a soul in him has quite as quaint fancies as this one of August's.

So he got over his terror and his sobbing both, though he was so utterly in the dark. He did not feel cramped at all, because the stove was so large, and air he had in plenty, as it came through the fretwork running round the top. He was hungry again, and again nibbled with prudence at his loaf and his sausage. He could not at all tell the hour. Every time the train stopped and he heard the banging, stamping, shouting, and jangling of chains that went on, his heart seemed to jump up into his mouth. If they should find him out! Sometimes porters came and took away this case and the other, a sack here, a bale there, now a big bag, now a dead chamois. Every time the men trampled near him, and swore at each other, and banged this and that to and fro, he was so frightened that his very breath seemed to stop. When they came to lift the stove out, would they find him? And if they did find him, would they kill him? That was what he kept thinking of all the way, all through the dark hours, which seemed without end.

Goods trains are usually very slow because of the stops, and are many days doing what a quick train does in a few hours. This one was quicker than most, because it was bearing goods to the King of Bavaria; still it took all the short winter's day and the long winter's night and half another day to go over ground that the mail trains cover in a forenoon. It passed great armored Kuffstein standing across the beautiful and solemn gorge, denying the right of way to all the foes of Austria. It passed twelve hours later, after lying by in out-of-the-way stations, pretty Rosenheim, that marks the border of Bavaria. And here the Nürnberg stove, with August inside it, was lifted out heedfully and set under a covered way. When it was lifted out, the boy had hard work to keep in his screams; he was tossed to and fro as the men lifted the huge thing, and the earthenware walls of his beloved fire-king were not cushions of down. However, though they swore and grumbled at the weight of it, they never suspected that a living child was inside it, and they carried it out onto the platform and set it down under the roof of the goods shed. There it passed the rest of the night and all the next morning, and August was all the while within.

The winds of early winter sweep bitterly over Rosenheim, and all the vast Bavarian plain was one white sheet of snow. If there had not been whole armies of men at work always clearing the iron rails of the snow, no trains could ever have run at all. Happily for August, the thick wrappings in which the stove was enveloped and the stoutness of its own make screened him from the cold, of which, else, he must have died—frozen. He had still some of his loaf, and a little—a very little—of his sausage. What he did begin to suffer from was thirst; and this frightened him almost more than anything else, for Dorothea had read aloud to them one night a story of the tortures some wrecked men had endured because they could not find any water but the salt sea. It was many hours since he had last taken a drink from the wooden spout of their old pump, which brought them the sparkling, ice-cold water of the hills.

But, fortunately for him, the stove, having been marked and registered as "fragile and valuable," was not treated quite like a mere bale of goods, and the Rosenheim station master, who knew its consignees, resolved to send it on by a passenger train that would leave there at daybreak. And when this train went out, in it, among piles of luggage belonging to other travelers, to Vienna, Prague, Budapest, Salzburg, was August, still undiscovered, still doubled up like a mole in the winter under the grass. Those words, "fragile and valuable," had made the men lift Hirschvogel gently and with care. He had begun to get used to his prison, and a little used to the incessant pounding and jumbling and rattling and shaking with which modern travel is always accompanied, though modern invention does deem itself so mightily clever. All in the dark he was, and he was terribly thirsty; but he kept feeling the earthenware sides of the Nürnberg giant and saying, softly, "Take care of me; oh, take care of me, dear Hirschvogel!"

He did not say, "Take me back;" for, now that he was fairly out in the world, he wished to see a little of it. He began to think that they must have been all over the world in all this time that the rolling and roaring and hissing and jangling had been about his ears shut up in the dark. He began to remember the tales that had been told in Yule round the fire at his grandfather's good house at Dorf, of gnomes and elves and subterranean terrors, and the Erl King riding on the black horse of night, and—and—and he began to sob and to tremble again, and this time did scream outright. But the steam was screaming itself so loudly that no one, had there been anyone nigh, would have heard him; and in another minute or so the train stopped with a jar and a jerk, and he in his cage could hear men crying aloud, "München! München!"

Then he knew enough of geography to know that he was in the heart of Bavaria. He had had an uncle killed in the Bayerischenwald by the Bavarian forest guards, when in the excitement of hunting a black bear he had overpassed the limits of the Tyrol frontier.

That fate of his kinsman, a gallant young chamois hunter who had taught him to handle a trigger and load a muzzle, made the very name of Bavaria a terror to August.

"It is Bavaria! It is Bavaria!" he sobbed to the stove; but the stove said nothing to him; it had no fire in it. A stove can no more speak without fire than a man can see without light. Give it fire, and it will sing to you, tell tales to you, offer you in return all the sympathy you ask.

"It is Bavaria!" sobbed August; for it is always a name of dread augury to the Tyroleans, by reason of those bitter struggles and midnight shots and untimely deaths which come from those meetings of jäger and hunter in the Bayerischenwald. But the train stopped: Munich was reached, and August, hot and cold by turns, and shaking like a little aspen leaf, felt himself once more carried out on the shoulders of men, rolled along on a truck, and finally set down, where he knew not, only he knew he was thirsty—so thirsty! If only he could have reached his hand out and scooped up a little snow!

He thought he had been moved on this truck many miles, but in truth the stove had been only taken from the railway station to a shop in the Marienplatz. Fortunately, the stove was always set upright on its four gilded feet, a junction to that effect having been affixed to its written label, and on its gilded feet it stood now in the small dark curiosity shop of one Hans Rhilfer.

"I shall not unpack it till Anton comes," he heard a man's voice say; and then he heard a key grate in a lock, and by the unbroken stillness that ensued he concluded he was alone, and ventured to peep through the straw and hay. What he saw was a small square room filled with pots and pans, pictures, carvings, old blue jugs, old steel armor, shields, daggers, Chinese idols, Vienna china, Turkish rugs, and all the art lumber and fabricated rubbish of a *bric-à-brac* dealer's. It seemed a wonderful place to him; but, oh! was there one drop of water in it all? That was his single thought; for his tongue was parching, and his throat felt on fire, and his chest began to be dry and choked as with dust. There was not a drop of water, but there was a lattice window grated, and beyond the window was a wide stone ledge covered with snow. August cast one look at the locked door, darted out of his hiding place, ran and opened the window, crammed the snow into his mouth again and again, and then flew back into the stove, drew the hay and straw over the place he entered by, tied the cords, and shut the brass door down on himself. He had brought some big icicles in with him, and by them his thirst was finally, if only temporarily, quenched. Then he sat still in the bottom of the stove, listening intently, wide awake, and once more recovering his natural boldness.

The thought of Dorothea kept nipping his heart and his conscience with a hard squeeze now and then, but he thought to himself, "If I can take her back Hirschvogel, then how pleased she will be, and how little 'Gilda will clap her hands!" He was not at all selfish in his love for Hirschvogel: he wanted it for them all at home quite as much as for himself. There was at the bottom of his mind a kind of ache of shame that his father—his own father—should have stripped their hearth and sold their honor thus.

A robin had been perched upon a stone griffin sculptured on a house-eave near. August had felt for the crumbs of his loaf in his pocket, and had thrown them to the little bird sitting so easily on the frozen snow.

In the darkness where he was he now heard a little song, made faint by the stove wall and the window-glass that was between him and it, but still distinct and exquisitely sweet. It was the robin, singing after feeding on the crumbs. August, as he heard, burst into tears. He thought of Dorothea, who every morning threw out some grain or some bread on the snow before the church. "What use is it going *there*," she said, "if we forget the sweetest creatures God has made?" Poor Dorothea! Poor, good, tender, much-burdened little soul! He thought of her till his tears ran like rain.

Yet it never once occurred to him to dream of going home. Hirschvogel was here.

Presently the key turned in the lock of the door, he heard heavy footsteps and the voice of the man who had said to his father, "You have a little mad dog; muzzle him!" The voice said, "Ay, ay, you have called me a fool many times. Now you shall see what I have gotten for two hundred dirty florins. *Potztausend!* never did *you* do such a stroke of work."

Then the other voice grumbled and swore, and the steps of the two men approached more closely, and the heart of the child went pit-a-pat, pit-a-pat, as a mouse's does when it is on the top of a cheese and hears a housemaid's broom sweeping near. They began to strip the stove of its wrappings: that he could tell by the noise they made with the hay and the straw. Soon they had stripped it wholly: that, too, he knew by the oaths and exclamations of wonder and surprise and rapture which broke from the man who had not seen it before.

"A right royal thing! A wonderful and never-to-be-rivaled thing! Grander than the great stove of Hohen-Salzburg! Sublime! Magnificent! Matchless!"

So the epithets ran on in thick guttural voices, diffusing a smell of lager beer so strong as they spoke that it reached August crouching in his stronghold. If they should open the door of the stove! That was his frantic fear. If they should open it, it would be all over with him. They would drag him out; most likely they would kill him, he thought, as his mother's young brother had been killed in the Wald.

The perspiration rolled off his forehead in his agony; but he had control enough over himself to keep quiet, and after standing by the Nürnberg master's work for nigh an hour, praising, marveling, expatiating in the lengthy German tongue, the men moved to a little distance and began talking of sums of money and divided profits, of which discourse he could make out no meaning. All he could make out was that the name of the king—the king—the king came over very often in their arguments. He fancied at times they quarrelled, for they swore lustily and their voices rose hoarse and high; but after a while they seemed to pacify each other and agree to something, and were in great glee, and so in these merry spirits came and slapped the luminous sides of stately Hirschvogel, and shouted to it—

"Old Mumchance, you have brought us rare good luck! To think you were smoking in a silly fool of a salt-baker's kitchen all these years!"

Then inside the stove August jumped up, with flaming cheeks and clinching hands, and was almost on the point of shouting out to them that they were the thieves and should say no evil of his father, when he remembered, just in time, that to breathe a word or make a sound was to bring ruin on himself and sever him forever from Hirschvogel. So he kept quite still, and the men barred the shutters of the little lattice and went out by the door, double locking it after them. He had made out from their talk that they were going to show Hirschvogel to some great person: therefore he kept quite still and dared not move.

Muffled sounds came to him through the shutters from the streets below—the rolling of wheels, the clanging of church bells, and bursts of that military music which is so seldom silent in the streets of Munich. An hour perhaps passed by; sounds of steps on the stairs kept him in perpetual apprehension. In the intensity of his anxiety, he forgot that he was hungry and many miles away from cheerful, Old World little Hall, lying by the clear gray river water, with the ramparts of the mountains all around.

Presently the door opened again sharply. He could hear the two dealers' voices murmuring unctuous words, in which "honor," "gratitude," and many fine long noble titles played the chief parts. The voice of another person, more clear and refined than theirs, answered them curtly, and then, close by the Nürnberg stove and the boy's ear, ejaculated a single *"Wunderschön!"* August almost lost his terror for himself in his thrill of pride at his beloved Hirschvogel being thus admired in the great city. He thought the master-potter must be glad too.

"Wunderschön!" ejaculated the stranger a second time, and then examined the stove in all its parts, read all its mottoes, gazed long on all its devices.

"It must have been made for the Emperor Maximilian," he said at last; and the poor little boy, meanwhile, within, was "hugged up into nothing," as you children say, dreading that every moment he would open the stove. And open it truly he did, and examined the brasswork of the door; but inside it was so dark that crouching August passed unnoticed, screwed up into a ball like a hedgehog as he was.   The gentleman shut the door at length, without having seen anything strange inside it; and then he talked long and low with the tradesmen, and, as his accent was different from that which August was used to, the child could distinguish little that he said, except the name of the king and the word "gulden" again and again. After a while he went away, one of the dealers accompanying him, one of them lingering behind to bar up the shutters.   Then this one also withdrew again, double locking the door.

The poor little hedgehog uncurled itself and dared to breathe aloud.

What time was it?

Late in the day, he thought, for to accompany the stranger they had lighted a lamp; he had heard the scratch of the match, and through the brass fretwork had seen the lines of light.

He would have to pass the night here, that was certain. He and Hirschvogel were locked in, but at least they were together.   If only he could have had something to eat! He thought with a pang of how at this hour at home they ate the sweet soup, sometimes with apples in it from Aunt Maïla's farm orchard, and sang together, and listened to Dorothea's reading of little tales, and basked in the glow and delight that had beamed on them from the great Nürnberg fire-king.

"Oh, poor, poor little 'Gilda!   What is she doing without dear Hirschvogel?" he thought.   Poor little 'Gilda! she had only now the black iron stove of the ugly little kitchen.   Oh, how cruel of father!

August could not bear to hear the dealers blame or laugh at his father, but he did feel that it had been so, so cruel to sell Hirschvogel.   The mere memory of all those long winter evenings, when they had all closed round it,

and roasted chestnuts or crabapples in it, and listened to
the howling of the wind and the deep sound of the church
bells, and tried very much to make each other believe that
the wolves still came down from the mountains into the
streets of Hall, and were that very minute growling at
the house door—all this memory coming on him with the
sound of the city bells, and the knowledge that night drew
near upon him so completely, being added to his hunger
and his fear, so overcame him that he burst out crying for
the fiftieth time since he had been inside the stove, and felt
that he would starve to death, and wondered dreamily if
Hirschvogel would care. Yes, he was sure Hirschvogel
would care. Had he not decked it all summer long with
alpine roses and edelweiss and heaths and made it sweet
with thyme and honeysuckle and great garden lilies?
Had he ever forgotten when Santa Claus came to make it
its crown of holly and ivy and wreathe it all around?

"Oh, shelter me; save me; take care of me!" he prayed
to the old fire-king, and forgot, poor little man, that he
had come on this wild-goose chase northward to save and
take care of Hirschvogel!

After a time he dropped asleep, as children can do
when they weep, and little robust hill-born boys most
surely do, be they where they may. It was not very cold
in this lumber-room; it was tightly shut up, and very full
of things, and at the back of it were the hot pipes of an
adjacent house, where a great deal of fuel was burnt.
Moreover, August's clothes were warm ones and his
blood was young. So he was not cold, though Munich is
terribly cold in the nights of December; and he slept on
and on—which was a comfort to him, for he forgot his
woes, and his perils, and his hunger, for a time.

Midnight was once more chiming from all the brazen
tongues of the city when he awoke, and, all being still

around him, ventured to put his head out of the brass door of the stove to see why such a strange bright light was round him.

It was a very strange and brilliant light indeed; and yet, what is perhaps still stranger, it did not frighten or amaze him, nor did what he saw alarm him either, and yet I think it would have done you or me. For what he saw was nothing less than all the *bric-à-brac* in motion.

A big jug, an Apostel-Krug, of Kruessen, was solemnly dancing a minuet with a plump Faenza jar. A tall Dutch clock was going through a gavotte with a spindle legged ancient chair. A very droll porcelain figure of Littenhausen was bowing to a very stiff soldier in *terre cuite* of Ulm. An old violin of Cremona was playing itself, and a queer little shrill plaintive music that thought itself merry came from a painted spinnet covered with faded roses. Some gilt Spanish leather had got up on the wall and laughed. A Dresden mirror was tripping about, crowned with flowers, and a Japanese bonze was riding along on a griffin. A slim Venetian rapier had come to blows with a stout Ferrara saber, all about a little pale-faced chit of a damsel in white Nymphenburg china. And a portly Franconian pitcher in *grès gris* was calling aloud, "Oh, these Italians! always at feud!" But nobody listened to him at all. A great number of little Dresden cups and saucers were all skipping and waltzing; the teapots, with their broad round faces, were spinning their own lids like teetotums. The high-backed gilded chairs were having a game of cards together; and a little Saxe poodle, with a blue ribbon at its throat, was running from one to another, whilst a yellow cat of Cornelis Lachtleven's rode about on a Delft horse in blue pottery of 1489. Meanwhile the brilliant light shed on the scene came from three silver candelabra, though they had no candles set up in them. And, what is the greatest miracle of all, August looked on at these mad freaks and felt no sensation of wonder! He only, as he heard the violin and the spinnet playing, felt an irresistible desire to dance too.

No doubt his face said what he wished; for a lovely little lady, all in pink and gold and white, with powdered hair, and high-heeled shoes, and all made of the very finest and fairest Meissen china, tripped up to him, and smiled, and gave him her hand and led him out to a minuet. And he danced it perfectly—poor little August in his thick, clumsy shoes and his thick, clumsy sheepskin jacket, and his rough homespun linen, and his broad Tyrolean hat! He must have danced it perfectly, this dance of kings and queens in days when crowns were duly honored, for the lovely lady always smiled benignly and never scolded him at all, and danced so divinely herself to the stately measures the spinnet was playing that August could not take his eyes off her till, their minuet ended, she sat down on her own white-and-gold bracket.

"I am the Princess of Saxe-Royale," she said to him, with a benignant smile; "and you have got through that minuet very fairly."

Then he ventured to say to her—

"Madame my princess, could you tell me kindly why some of the figures and furniture dance and speak, and some lie up in a corner like lumber? It does make me curious. Is it rude to ask?"

For it greatly puzzled him why, when some of the *bric-à-brac* was all full of life and motion, some was quite still and had not a single thrill in it.

"My dear child," said the powdered lady, "is it possible that you do not know the reason? Why, those silent, dull things are *imitation!*"

This she said with so much decision that she evidently considered it a condensed but complete answer.

"Imitation?" repeated August, timidly, not understanding.

"Of course! Lies, falsehoods, fabrications!" said the princess in pink shoes, very vivaciously. "They only *pretend* to be what we *are!* They never wake up:how can they? No imitation ever had any soul in it yet."

"Oh!" said August humbly, not even sure that he understood entirely yet. He looked at Hirschvogel; surely it had a royal soul within it: would it not wake up and speak? Oh dear! how he longed to hear the voice of his fire-king! And he began to forget that he stood by a lady who sat upon a pedestal of gold-and-white china, with the year 1746 cut on it, and the Meissen mark.

"What will you be when you are a man?" said the little lady sharply, for her black eyes were quick though her red lips were smiling. "Will you work for the *Königliche Porcellan-Manufactur,* like my great dead Kandler?"

"I have never thought," said August, stammering, "at least—that is—I do wish—I do hope to be a painter, as was Master Augustin Hirschvogel at Nürnberg."

"Bravo!" said all the real *bric-à-brac* in one breath, and the two Italian rapiers left off their fighting to cry, *"Ben-one!"* For there is not a bit of true *bric-à-brac* in all Europe that does not know the names of the mighty masters.

August felt quite pleased to have won so much applause, and grew as red as the lady's shoes with bashful contentment.

"I knew all the Hirschvögel, from old Veit downwards," said a fat *grès de Flandre* beer jug: "I myself was made at Nürnberg." And he bowed to the great stove

very politely, taking off his own silver hat—I mean lid—
with a courtly sweep that he could scarcely have learned
from burgomasters. The stove, however, was silent, and
a sickening suspicion (for what is such heartbreak as a
suspicion of what we love?) came through the mind of
August: *Was Hirschvogel only imitation?*

"No, no, no, no!" he said to himself stoutly: though
Hirschvogel never stirred, never spoke, yet would he keep
all faith in it. After all their happy years together, after
all the nights of warmth and joy he owed it, should he
doubt his own friend and hero, whose gilt lion's feet he
had kissed in his babyhood? "No, no, no, no!" he said,
again, with so much emphasis that the Lady of Meissen
looked sharply again at him.

"No," she said, with pretty disdain, "no, believe me,
they may 'pretend' forever. They can never look like us!
They imitate even our marks, but never can they look like
the real thing, never can they *chassent de race.*"

"How should they?" said a bronze statuette of
Vischer's. "They daub themselves green with verdigris,
or sit out in the rain to get rusted; but green and rust are
not *patina;* only the ages can give that!"

"And *my* imitations are all in primary colors, staring
colors, hot as the colors of a hostelry's signboard!" said
the Lady of Meissen, with a shiver.

"Well, there is a *grès de Flandre* over there, who
pretends to be a Hans Kraut, as I am," said the jug with
the silver hat, pointing with his handle to a jug that lay
prone on its side in a corner. "He has copied me as
exactly as it is given to moderns to copy us. Almost he
might be mistaken for me. But yet what a difference
there is! How crude are his blues! how evidently done
over the glaze are his black letters! He has tried to give
himself my very twist; but what a lamentable exaggera-

tion of that playful deviation in my lines which in his becomes actual deformity!"

"And look at that," said the gilt Cordovan leather with a contemptuous glance at a broad piece of gilded leather spread out on a table. "They will sell him cheek by jowl with me, and give him my name; but look! *I* am overlaid with pure gold beaten thin as a film and laid on me in absolute honesty by worthy Diego de las Gorgias, worker in leather of lovely Cordova in the blessed reign of Ferdinand the Most Christian. *His* gilding is one part gold to eleven other parts of brass and rubbish, and it has been laid on him with a brush—*a brush!*—pah! of course he will be as black as a crock in a few years' time, while I am as bright as when I first was made, and, unless I am burnt as my Cordova burnt its heretics, I shall shine on forever."

"They carve pearwood because it is so soft, and dye it brown, and call it *me!*" said an old oak cabinet, with a chuckle.

"That is not so painful; it does not vulgarize you so much as the cups they paint today and christen after *me!*" said a Carl Theodor cup subdued in hue, yet gorgeous as a jewel.

"Nothing can be so annoying as to see common gimcracks aping *me!*" interposed the princess in the pink shoes.

"They even steal my motto, though it is Scripture," said a *Trauerkrug* of Regensburg in black-and-white.

"And my own dots they put on plain English china creatures!" sighed the little white maid of Nymphenburg.

"And they sell hundreds and thousands of common china plates, calling them after me, and baking my saints and my legends in a muffle of today; it is blasphemy!" said a stout plate of Gubbio, which in its year of birth had seen the face of Maestro Giorgio.

"That is what is so terrible in these *bric-à-brac* places," said the princess of Meissen. "It brings one in contact with such low, imitative creatures; one really is safe nowhere nowadays unless under glass at the Louvre or South Kensington."

"And they get even there," sighed the *grès de Flandre*. "A terrible thing happened to a dear friend of mine, a *terre cuite* of Blasius (you know the *terres cuites* of Blasius date from 1560). Well, he was put under glass in a museum that shall be nameless, and he found himself set next to his own imitation born and baked yesterday at Frankfort, and what think you the miserable creature said to him, with a grin? 'Old Pipeclay,'—that is what he called my friend—'the fellow that bought *me* got just as much commission on me as the fellow that bought *you*, and that was all that *he* thought about. You know it is only the public money that goes!' And the horrid creature grinned again till he actually cracked himself. There is a Providence above all things, even museums."

"Providence might have interfered before, and saved the public money," said the little Meissen lady.

"After all, does it matter?" said a Dutch jar of Haarlem. "All the shamming in the world will not *make* them us!"

"One does not like to be vulgarized," said the Lady of Meissen angrily.

"My maker, the Krabbetje,* did not trouble his head about that," said the Haarlem jar proudly. "The Krabbetje made me for the kitchen, the bright, clean,

---

* Jan Asselyn, called Krabbetje, the little Crab, born 1610, master-potter of Delft and Haarlem.

snow-white Dutch kitchen, well nigh three centuries ago, and now I am thought worthy the palace; yet I wish I were at home; yet, I wish I could see the good Dutch vrouw, and the shining canals, and the great green meadows dotted with the kine."

"Ah! if we could all go back to our makers!" sighed the Gubbio plate, thinking of the Giorgio Andreoli and the glad and gracious days of the Renaissance: and somehow the words touched the frolicsome souls of the dancing jars, the spinning teapots, the chairs that were playing cards; and the violin stopped its merry music with a sob, and the spinnet sighed—thinking of dead hands.

Even the little Saxe poodle howled for a master forever lost; and only the swords went on quarreling, and made such a clattering noise that the Japanese bonze rode at them on his monster and knocked them both right over, and they lay straight and still, looking foolish, and the little Nymphenburg maid, though she was crying, smiled and almost laughed.

Then from where the great stove stood there came a solemn voice.

All eyes turned upon Hirschvogel, and the heart of its little human comrade gave a great jump of joy.

"My friends," said that clear voice from the turret of Nürnberg faïence, "I have listened to all you have said. There is too much talking among the Mortalities whom one of themselves has called the Windbags. Let not us be like them. I hear among men so much vain speech, so much precious breath and precious time wasted in empty boasts, foolish anger, useless reiteration, blatant argument, ignoble mouthings, that I have learned to deem speech a curse, laid on man to weaken and envenom all his undertakings. For over two hundred years I have never spoken myself: you, I hear, are not so reticent. I only speak now because one of you said a beautiful thing that touched me. If we all might but go back to our makers! Ah, yes! if we might! We were made in days when even men were true creatures, and so we, the work of their hands, were true too. We, the begotten of ancient days, derive all the value in us from the fact that our makers wrought at us with zeal, with piety, with integrity, with faith—not to win fortunes or to glut a market, but to do nobly an honest thing and create for the honor of the Arts and God.

"I see there is here amidst you a little human thing who loves me, and in his own ignorant childish way loves Art. Now, I want him forever to remember this night and these words; to remember that we are what we are, and precious in the eyes of the world, because centuries ago those who were of single mind and of pure hand so created us, scorning sham and haste and counterfeit. Well do I recollect my master, Augustin Hirschvogel. He led a wise and blameless life, and wrought in loyalty and love, and made his time beautiful thereby, like one of his own rich, many-colored church casements, that told holy tales as the sun streamed through them. Ah, yes, my friends, to go back to our masters!—that would be the best that could befall us. But they are gone, and even the perishable labors of their lives outlive them. For many, many years I, once honored of emperors, dwelt in a humble house and warmed in successive winters three generations of little, cold, hungry children. When I warmed them they forgot that they were hungry; they laughed and told tales, and slept at last about my feet. Then I knew that humble as had become my lot it was one that my master would have wished for me, and I was content. Sometimes a tired woman would creep up to me, and smile because she was near me, and point out my golden crown or my ruddy fruit to a baby in her arms. That was better than to stand in a great hall of a great city, cold and empty, even though wise men came to gaze and throngs of fools gaped, passing with flattering words. Where I go now I know not; but since I go from that humble house where they loved me, I shall be sad and alone. They pass so soon—those fleeting mortal lives! Only we endure— we, the things that the human brain creates. We can but bless them a little as they glide by: if we have done that, we have done what our masters wished. So in us our masters, being dead, yet may speak and live."

Then the voice sank away in silence, and a strange golden light that had shone on the great stove faded away; so also the light died down in the silver candelabra. A soft, pathetic melody stole gently through the room. It came from the old, old spinnet that was covered with the faded roses.

Then that sad, sighing music of a bygone day died too; the clocks of the city struck six of the morning; day was rising over the Bayerischenwald. August awoke with a great start, and found himself lying on the bare bricks of the floor of the chamber, and all the *bric-à-brac* was lying quite still all around. The pretty Lady of Meissen was motionless on her porcelain bracket, and the little Saxe poodle was quiet at her side.

August rose slowly to his feet. He was very cold, but he was not sensible of it or of the hunger that was gnawing his little empty entrails. He was absorbed in the wondrous sight, in the wondrous sounds, that he had seen and heard.

All was dark around him. Was it still midnight or had morning come? Morning, surely; for against the barred shutters he heard the tiny song of the robin.

Tramp, tramp, too, came a heavy step up the stair. He

had but a moment in which to scramble back into the interior of the great stove, when the door opened and the two dealers entered, bringing burning candles with them to see their way.

August was scarcely conscious of danger more than he was of cold or hunger. A marvelous sense of courage, of security, of happiness, was about him, like strong and gentle arms enfolding him and lifting him upwards—upwards—upwards! Hirschvogel would defend him.

The dealers undid the shutters, scaring the redbreast away, and then tramped about in their heavy boots and chattered in contented voices, and began to wrap up the stove once more in all its straw and hay and cordage.

It never once occurred to them to glance inside. Why should they look inside a stove that they had bought and were about to sell again for all its glorious beauty of exterior?

The child did not feel afraid. A great exaltation had come to him: he was like one lifted up by his angels.

Presently the two traders called up their porters, and the stove, heedfully swathed and wrapped and tended as though it were some sick prince going on a journey, was borne on the shoulders of six stout Bavarians down the stairs and out of the door into the Marienplatz. Even behind all those wrappings August felt the icy bite of the intense cold of the outer air at dawn of a winter's day in Munich. The men moved the stove with exceeding gentleness and care, so that he had often been far more roughly shaken in his big brothers' arms than he was in his journey now; and though both hunger and thirst made themselves felt, being foes that will take no denial, he was still in that state of nervous exaltation which deadens all physical suffering and is at once a cordial and an opiate. He had heard Hirschvogel speak; that was enough.

It never once occurred to him to dream of going home

The stout carriers tramped through the city, six of them, with the Nürnberg fire-castle on their brawny shoulders, and went right across Munich to the railway station, and August in the dark recognized all the ugly, jangling, pounding, roaring, hissing railway noises, and thought, despite his courage and excitement, "Will it be a *very* long journey?" For his stomach had at times an odd sinking sensation, and his head sadly often felt light and swimming. If it was a very, very long journey he felt half afraid that he would be dead or something bad before the end, and Hirschvogel would be so lonely: that was what he thought most about; not much about himself, and not much about Dorothea and the house at home. He was "high strung to high emprise," and could not look behind him.

Whether for a long or a short journey, whether for weal or woe, the stove with August still within it was once more hoisted up into a great van: but this time it was not all alone, and the two dealers as well as the six porters were all with it.

He in his darkness knew that, for he heard their voices. The train glided away over the Bavarian plain southward; and he heard the men say something of Berg and the Wurm-See, but their German was strange to him, and he could not make out what these names meant.

The train rolled on, with all its fume and fuss, and roar of steam, and stench of oil and burning coal. It had to go quietly and slowly on account of the snow which was falling, and which had fallen all night.

"He might have waited till he came to the city," grumbled one man to another. "What weather to stay on at Berg!"

But who he was that stayed on at Berg, August could not make out at all.

Though the men grumbled about the state of the roads and the season, they were hilarious and well content, for they laughed often, and, when they swore, did so good-humoredly, and promised their porters fine presents at New Year; and August, like a shrewd little boy as he was, who even in the secluded Innthal had learned that money is the chief mover of men's mirth, thought to himself, with a terrible pang—

"They have sold Hirschvogel for some great sum! They have sold him already!"

Then his heart grew faint and sick within him, for he knew very well that he must soon die, shut up without food and water thus; and what new owner of the great fireplace would ever permit him to dwell in it?

"Never mind, I *will* die," thought he, "and Hirschvogel will know it."

Perhaps you think him a very foolish little fellow, but I do not.

It is good to be loyal and ready to endure to the end.

It is but an hour and a quarter that the train usually takes to pass from Munich to the Wurm-See or Lake of Starnberg; but this morning the journey was much slower, because the way was encumbered by snow. When it did reach Possenhofen and stop, and the Nürnberg stove was lifted out once more, August could see through the fret-work of the brass door, as the stove stood upright facing the lake, that this Wurm-See was a calm and noble piece of water, of great width, with low wooded banks and distant mountains, a peaceful, serene place, full of rest.

It was now near ten o'clock. The sun had come forth; there was a clear gray sky hereabouts; the snow was not falling, though it lay white and smooth everywhere, down to the edge of the water, which before long would itself be ice.

Before he had time to get more than a glimpse of the green gliding surface, the stove was again lifted up and placed on a large boat that was in waiting—one of those very long and huge boats which the women in these parts use as laundries, and the men as timber rafts. The stove, with much labor and much expenditure of time and care, was hoisted into this, and August would have grown sick and giddy with the heaving and falling if his big brothers had not long used him to such tossing about, so that he was as much at ease head, as feet, downward. The stove once in it safely with its guardians, the big boat moved across the lake to Leoni. How a little hamlet on a Bavarian lake got that Tuscan-sounding name I cannot tell; but Leoni it is. The big boat was a long time crossing: the lake here is about three miles broad, and these heavy barges are unwieldy and heavy to move, even though they are towed and tugged at from the shore.

"If we should be too late!" the two dealers muttered to each other, in agitation and alarm. "He said eleven o'clock."

"Who was he?" thought August. "The buyer, of course, of Hirschvogel." The slow passage across the Wurm-See was accomplished at length: the lake was placid; there was a sweet calm in the air and on the water; there was a great deal of snow in the sky, though the sun was shining and gave a solemn hush to the atmosphere. Boats and one little steamer were going up and down; in the clear frosty light the distant mountains of Zillerthal and the Algau Alps were visible; market people, cloaked and furred, went by on the water or on the banks; the deep woods of the shores were black and gray and brown. Poor August could see nothing of a scene that would have delighted him; as the stove was now set, he could only see the old worm-eaten wood of the huge barge.

Presently they touched the pier at Leoni.

"Now men, for a stout mile and a half! You shall drink your reward at Christmas time," said one of the dealers to his porters, who, stout, strong men as they were, showed a disposition to grumble at their task. Encouraged by large promises, they shouldered sullenly the Nürnberg stove, grumbling again at its preposterous weight, but little dreaming that they carried within it a small, panting, trembling boy; for August began to tremble now that he was about to see the future owner of Hirschvogel.

"If he look a good, kind man," he thought, "I will beg him to let me stay with it."

The porters began their toilsome journey, and moved off from the village pier. He could see nothing, for the brass door was over his head, and all that gleamed through it was the clear gray sky. He had been tilted onto his back, and if he had not been a little mountaineer, used to hanging head downwards over crevasses, and, moreover, seasoned to rough treatment by the hunters and guides of the hills and the salt-workers in the town, he would have been made ill and sick by the bruising and shaking and many changes of position to which he had been subjected.

The way the men took was a mile and a half in length, but the road was heavy with snow, and the burden they bore was heavier still. The dealers cheered them on, swore at them and praised them in one breath; besought them and reiterated their splendid promises, for a clock was striking eleven, and they had been ordered to reach their destination at that hour, and, though the air was so cold, the heat drops rolled off their foreheads as they walked, they were so frightened at being late. But the porters would not budge a foot quicker than they chose,

and as they were not poor four-footed carriers their em-
ployers dared not thrash them, though most willingly
would they have done so.

The road seemed terribly long to the anxious tradesmen, to the plodding porters, to the poor little man inside
the stove, as he kept sinking and rising, sinking and rising,
with each of their steps.

Where they were going he had no idea, only after a
very long time he lost the sense of the fresh icy wind
blowing on his face through the brass work above, and
felt by their movements beneath him that they were
mounting steps or stairs. Then he heard a great many
different voices, but he could not understand what was
being said. He felt that his bearers paused some time,
then moved on and on again. Their feet went so softly he
thought they must be moving on carpet, and as he felt a
warm air come to him he concluded that he was in some
heated chambers, for he was a clever little fellow, and
could put two and two together, though he was so hungry
and so thirsty and his empty stomach felt so strangely.
They must have gone, he thought, through some very
great number of rooms, for they walked so long on and
on, on and on. At last the stove was set down again, and,
happily for him, set so that his feet were downward.

What he fancied was that he was in some museum, like
that which he had seen in the city of Innspruck.

The voices he heard were very hushed, and the steps
seemed to go away, far away, leaving him alone with
Hirschvogel. He dared not look out, but he peeped
through the brass work, and all he could see was a big
carved lion's head in ivory, with a gold crown atop. It
belonged to a velvet fauteuil, but he could not see the
chair, only the ivory lion.

There was a delicious fragrance in the air—a fragrance

as of flowers. "Only how can it be flowers?" thought August. "It is November!"

From afar off, as it seemed, there came a dreamy, exquisite music, as sweet as the spinnet's had been, but so much fuller, so much richer, seeming as though a chorus of angels were singing all together. August ceased to think of the museum: he thought of heaven. "Are we gone to the Master?" he thought, remembering the words of Hirschvogel.

All was so still around him; there was no sound anywhere except the sound of the far-off choral music.

He did not know it, but he was in the royal castle of Berg, and the music he heard was the music of Wagner, who was playing in a distant room some of the motifs of "Parsifal."

Presently he heard a fresh step near him, and he heard a low voice say, close behind him, "So!" An exclamation no doubt, he thought, of admiration and wonder at the beauty of Hirschvogel.

Then the same voice said, after a long pause, during which no doubt, as August thought, this newcomer was examining all the details of the wondrous fire-tower, "It was well bought; it is exceedingly beautiful! It is most undoubtedly the work of Augustin Hirschvogel."

Then the hand of the speaker turned the round handle of the brass door, and the fainting soul of the poor little prisoner within grew sick with fear.

The handle turned, the door was slowly drawn open, someone bent down and looked in, and the same voice that he had heard in praise of its beauty called aloud, in surprise, "What is this in it? A live child!"

Then August, terrified beyond all self-control, and dominated by one master passion, sprang out of the body of the stove and fell at the feet of the speaker.

"Oh, let me stay! Pray, meinherr, let me stay!" he sobbed. "I have come all the way with Hirschvogel!"

Some gentlemen's hands seized him, not gently by any means, and their lips angrily muttered in his ear, "Little knave, peace! Be quiet! Hold your tongue! It is the king!"

They were about to drag him out of the august atmosphere as if he had been some venomous, dangerous beast come there to slay, but the voice he had heard speak of the stove said, in kind accents, "Poor little child! He is very young. Let him go. Let him speak to me."

The word of a king is law to his courtiers: so, sorely against their wish, the angry and astonished chamberlains let August slide out of their grasp, and he stood there in his little rough sheepskin coat and his thick, mud-covered boots, with his curling hair all in a tangle, in the midst of the most beautiful chamber he had ever dreamed of, and in the presence of a young man with a beautiful dark face, and eyes full of dreams and fire; and the young man said to him, "My child, how came you here, hidden in this stove? Be not afraid: tell me the truth. I am the king."

August in an instinct of homage cast his great battered black hat with the tarnished gold tassels down on the floor of the room, and folded his little brown hands in supplication. He was too intensely in earnest to be in any way abashed; he was too lifted out of himself by his love for Hirschvogel to be conscious of any awe before any earthly majesty. He was only so glad—so glad it was the king. Kings were always kind; so the Tyrolese think, who love their lords.

"Oh, dear king!" he said, with trembling entreaty in his faint little voice, "Hirschvogel was ours, and we have loved it all our lives; and father sold it. And when I saw that it did really go from us, then I said to myself I would go with it; and I have come all the way inside it. And last night it spoke and said beautiful things. And I do pray you to let me live with it, and I will go out every morning and cut wood for it and you, if only you will let me stay beside it. No one ever has fed it with fuel but me since I grew big enough, and it loves me—it does indeed; it said so last night; and it said it had been happier with us than if it were in any palace——"

And then his breath failed him, and, as he lifted his little eager, pale face to the young king's, great tears were falling down his cheeks.

Now, the king likes all poetic and uncommon things, and there was that in the child's face which pleased and touched him. He motioned to his gentlemen to leave the little boy alone.

"What is your name?" he asked him.

"I am August Strehla. My father is Karl Strehla. We live in Hall in the Innthal; and Hirschvogel has been ours so long—so long!"

His lips quivered with a broken sob.

"And have you truly traveled inside this stove all the way from Tyrol?"

"Yes," said August. "No one thought to look inside till you did."

The king laughed; then another view of the matter occurred to him.

"Who bought the stove of your father?" he inquired.

"Traders of Munich," said August, who did not know that he ought not to have spoken to the king as to a simple citizen, and whose little brain was whirling and spinning dizzily round its one central idea.

"What sum did they pay your father, do you know?" asked the sovereign.

"Two hundred florins," said August, with a great sigh

of shame. "It was so much money, and he is so poor, and there are so many of us."

The king turned to his gentlemen-in-waiting. "Did these dealers of Munich come with the stove?"

He was answered in the affirmative. He desired them to be sought for and brought before him. As one of his chamberlains hastened on the errand, the monarch looked at August with compassion.

"You are very pale, little fellow: when did you eat last?"

"I had some bread and sausage with me; yesterday afternoon I finished it."

"You would like to eat now?"

"If I might have a little water I would be glad; my throat is very dry."

The king had water and wine brought for him, and cake also; but August, though he drank eagerly, could not swallow anything. His mind was in too great a tumult.

"May I stay with Hirschvogel?—may I stay?" he said, with feverish agitation.

"Wait a little," said the king, and asked abruptly. "What do you wish to be when you are a man?"

"A painter. I wish to be what Hirschvogel was—I mean the master that made *my* Hirschvogel."

"I understand," said the king.

Then the two dealers were brought into their sovereign's presence. They were so terribly alarmed, not being either so innocent or so ignorant as August was, that they were trembling as though they were being led to the slaughter, and they were so utterly astonished too at a child having come all the way from Tyrol in the stove, as a gentleman of the court had just told them this child had done, that they could not tell what to say or where to look, and presented a very foolish aspect indeed.

"Did you buy this Nürnberg stove of this little boy's father for two hundred florins?" the king asked them; and his voice was no longer soft and kind as it had been when addressing the child, but very stern.

"Yes, your majesty," murmured the trembling traders.

"And how much did the gentleman who purchased it for me give to you?"

"Two thousand ducats, your majesty," muttered the dealers, frightened out of their wits, and telling the truth in their fright.

The gentleman was not present: he was a trusted councilor in art matters of the king's, and often made purchases for him.

The king smiled a little and said nothing. The gentleman had made out the price to him as eleven thousand ducats.

"You will give at once to this boy's father the two thousand gold ducats that you received, less the two hundred Austrian florins that you paid him," said the king to his humiliated and abject subjects. "You are great rogues. Be thankful you are not more greatly punished."

He dismissed them by a sign to his courtiers, and to one of these gave the mission of making the dealers of the Marienplatz disgorge their ill-gotten gains.

August heard, and felt dazzled yet miserable. Two thousand gold Bavarian ducats for his father! Why, his father would never need to go any more to the salt baking! And yet, whether for ducats or for florins, Hirschvogel was sold just the same, and would the king let him stay with it—would he?

"Oh, do! Oh, please do!" he murmured, joining his little brown weather-stained hands, and kneeling down before the young monarch, who himself stood absorbed in painful thought, for the deception so basely practiced for the greedy sake of gain on him by a trusted councilor was bitter to him.   He looked down on the child, and as he did so smiled once more.

"Rise up, my little man," he said, in a kind voice. "Kneel only to your God.   Will I let you stay with your Hirschvogel?   Yes, I will; you shall stay at my court, and you shall be taught to be a painter—in oils or on porcelain as you will—and you must grow up worthily, and win all the laurels at our Schools of Art, and if when you are twenty-one years old you have done well and bravely, then I will give you your Nürnberg stove, or, if I am no more living, then those who reign after me shall do so.   And now go away with this gentleman, and be not afraid, and you shall light a fire every morning in Hirschvogel, but you will not need to go out and cut the wood."

Then he smiled and stretched out his hand.   The courtiers tried to make August understand that he ought to bow and touch it with his lips, but August could not understand that anyhow; he was too happy.   He threw his two arms about the king's knees, and kissed his feet passionately; then he lost all sense of where he was, and fainted away from hunger, and tiredness, and emotion, and wondrous joy.

As the darkness of his swoon closed in on him, he heard in his fancy the voice from Hirschvogel saying—

"Let us be worthy our maker!"

He is only a scholar yet, but he is a happy scholar, and promises to be a great man.   Sometimes he goes back for a few days to Hall, where the gold ducats have made his father prosperous.   In the old house-room there is a large white porcelain stove of Munich, the king's gift to Dorothea and 'Gilda.

And August never goes home without going into the great church and saying his thanks to God, who blessed his strange winter's journey in the Nürnberg stove. As for his dream in the dealers' room that night, he will never admit that he did dream it; he still declares that he saw it all, and heard the voice of Hirschvogel. And who shall say that he did not? For what is the gift of the poet and the artist except to see the sights which others cannot see and to hear the sounds that others cannot hear?

MOUFFLOU

Lolo wove the straw covering of wine flasks and plaited the cane matting with busy fingers

MOUFFLOU

MOUFFLOU'S masters were some boys and girls. They were very poor, but they were very merry. They lived in an old, dark, tumbledown place, and their father had been dead five years; their mother's care was all they knew; and Tasso was the eldest of them all, a lad of nearly twenty, and he was so kind, so good, so laborious, so cheerful, and so gentle, that the children all younger than he adored him. Tasso was a gardener. Tasso, however, though the eldest and mainly the breadwinner, was not so much Moufflou's master as was little Romolo, who was only ten, and a cripple. Romolo, called generally Lolo, had taught Moufflou all he knew; and that all was a very great deal, for nothing cleverer than was Moufflou had ever walked upon four legs.

Why Moufflou?

Well, when the poodle had been given to them by a soldier who was going back to his home in Piedmont, he had been a white woolly creature of a year old, and the children's mother, who was a Corsican by birth, had said that he was just like a *moufflon,* as they call sheep in Corsica. White and woolly this dog remained, and he became the handsomest and biggest poodle in all the city, and the corruption of Moufflou from Moufflon remained the name by which he was known; it was silly, perhaps, but it suited him and the children, and Moufflou he was.

They lived in an old quarter of Florence, in that picturesque zigzag which goes round the grand church of Or San Michele, and which is almost more Venetian than Tuscan in its mingling of color, charm, stateliness, popular confusion, and architectural majesty. The tall old houses are weather-beaten into the most delicious hues; the pavement is enchantingly encumbered with peddlers and stalls and all kinds of trades going on in the open air, in that bright, merry, beautiful Italian custom which, alas, alas! is being driven away by new-fangled laws which deem it better for the people to be stuffed up in close, stewing rooms without air, and would fain do away with all the good-tempered politics and the sensible philosophies and the wholesome chatter which the open-street trades and street gossipry encourage, for it is good for the populace to *sfogare* and in no other way can it do so one half so innocently. Drive it back into musty shops, and it is driven at once to mutter sedition. . . . But you want to hear about Moufflou.

Well, Moufflou lived here in that high house with the sign of the lamb in wrought iron, which shows it was once a warehouse of the old guild of the Arte della Lana. They are all old houses here, drawn round about that grand church which I called once, and will call again, like a mighty casket of oxidized silver. A mighty casket indeed, holding the Holy Spirit within it; and with the vermilion and the blue and the orange glowing in its niches and its lunettes like enamels, and its statues of the apostles strong and noble, like the times in which they were created—St. Peter with his keys, and St. Mark with his open book, and St. George leaning on his sword, and others also, solemn and austere as they, austere though benign, for do they not guard the White Tabernacle of Orcagna within?

The church stands firm as a rock, square as a fortress of stone, and the winds and the waters of the skies may beat about it as they will, they have no power to disturb its sublime repose. Sometimes I think of all the noble things in all our Italy Or San Michele is the noblest, standing there in its stern magnificence, amidst people's hurrying feet and noisy laughter, a memory of God.

The little masters of Moufflou lived right in its shadow, where the bridge of stone spans the space between the houses and the church high in midair: and little Lolo loved the church with a great love. He loved it in the morning-time, when the sunbeams turned it into dusky gold and jasper; he loved it in the evening-time, when the lights of its altars glimmered in the dark, and the scent of its incense came out into the street; he loved it in the great feasts, when the huge clusters of lilies were borne inside it; he loved it in the solemn nights of winter; the flickering gleam of the dull lamps shone on the robes of an apostle, or the sculpture of a shield, or the glow of a casement-molding in majolica. He loved it always, and, without knowing why, he called it *la mia chiesa*.

Lolo, being lame and of delicate health, was not enabled to go to school or to work, though he wove the straw covering of wine-flasks and plaited the cane matting with busy fingers. But for the most part he did as he liked, and spent most of his time sitting on the parapet of Or San Michele, watching the venders of earthenware at their trucks, or trotting with his crutch (and he could trot a good many miles when he chose) out with Moufflou down a bit of the Stocking-makers' Street, along under the arcades of the Uffizi, and so over the Jewelers' Bridge, and out by byways that he knew into the fields on the hillside upon the other bank of Arno. Moufflou and he would spend half the day—all the day—out there in daffodil time; and Lolo would come home with great bundles and sheaves of golden flowers, and he and Moufflou were happy.

His mother never liked to say a harsh word to Lolo, for he was lame through her fault: she had let him fall in his babyhood, and the mischief had been done to his hip never again to be undone. So she never raised her voice to him, though she did often to the others—to curly-pated Cecco, and pretty black-eyed Dina, and saucy Bice, and sturdy Beppo, and even to the good, manly, hard-working Tasso. Tasso was the mainstay of the whole, though he was but a gardener's lad, working in the green Cascine at small wages. But all he earned he brought home to his mother; and he alone kept in order the lazy, high-tempered Sandro, and he alone kept in check Bice's love of finery, and he alone could with shrewdness and care make both ends meet and put *minestra* always in the pot and bread always in the cupboard.

When his mother thought, as she thought indeed almost ceaselessly, that with a few months he would be of the age to draw his number, and might draw a high one and be taken from her for three years, the poor soul believed her very heart would burst and break; and many a day at twilight she would start out unperceived and creep into the great church and pour her soul forth in supplication before the White Tabernacle.

Yet, pray as she would, no miracle could happen to make Tasso free of military service: if he drew a fatal number, go he must, even though he take all the lives of them to their ruin with him.

One morning Lolo sat as usual on the parapet of the church, Moufflou beside him. It was a brilliant morning in September. The men at the handbarrows and at the stalls were selling the crockery, the silk handkerchiefs, and the straw hats which form the staple of the commerce that goes on round about Or San Michele—very blithe, good-natured, gay commerce, for the most part, not got through, however, of course, without bawling and screaming, and shouting and gesticulating, as if the sale of a penny pipkin or a twopenny pie pan were the occasion for the exchange of many thousands of pounds sterling and cause for the whole world's commotion. It was about eleven o'clock. The poor petitioners were going in for alms to the house of the fraternity of San Giovanni Battista. The barber at the corner was shaving a big man with a cloth tucked about his chin, and his chair set well out on the pavement. The sellers of the pipkins and pie pans were screaming till they were hoarse, "*Un soldo l'uno, due soldi tre!*" big bronze bells were booming till they seemed to clang right up to the deep blue sky; some brethren of the Misericordia went by bearing a black bier; a large sheaf of glowing flowers—dahlias, zinnias, asters, and daturas—was borne through the huge arched door of the church near St. Mark and his open book. Lolo looked on at it all, and so did Moufflou, and a stranger looked at them as he left the church.

"You have a handsome poodle there, my little man," he

said to Lolo, in a foreigner's too distinct and careful Italian.

"Moufflou is beautiful," said Lolo with pride. "You should see him when he is just washed; but we can only wash him on Sundays, because then Tasso is at home."

"How old is your dog?"

"Three years old."

"Does he do any tricks?"

"Does he!" said Lolo with a very derisive laugh. "Why, Moufflou can do anything! He can walk on two legs ever so long; make ready, present, and fire; die; waltz; beg, of course; shut a door; make a wheelbarrow of himself: there is nothing he will not do. Would you like to see him do something?"

"Very much," said the foreigner.

To Moufflou and to Lolo the street was the same thing as home; this cheery *piazzetta* by the church, so utterly empty sometimes, and sometimes so noisy and crowded, was but the wider threshold of their home to both the poodle and the child.

So there, under the lofty and stately walls of the old church, Lolo put Moufflou through his exercises. They were second nature to Moufflou, as to most poodles. He had inherited his address at them from clever parents, and, as he had never been frightened or coerced, all his lessons and acquirements were but play to him. He acquitted himself admirably, and the crockery venders came and looked on, and a sacristan came out of the church and smiled, and the barber left his customer's chin all in a lather while he laughed, for the good folk of the quarter were all proud of Moufflou and never tired of him, and the pleasant, easy-going, good-humored disposition of the Tuscan populace is so far removed from the stupid buckram and whalebone in which the new-fangled democracy wants to imprison it.

The stranger also was much diverted by Moufflou's talents, and said, half aloud, "How this clever dog would amuse poor Victor! Would you bring your poodle to please a sick child I have at home?" he said, quite aloud, to Lolo, who smiled and answered that he would. Where was the sick child?

"At the Gran Bretagna, not far off," said the gentleman. "Come this afternoon, and ask for me by this name."

He dropped his card and a couple of francs into Lolo's hand, and went his way. Lolo, with Moufflou scampering after him, dashed into his own house, and stumped up the stairs, his crutch making a terrible noise on the stone.

"Mother, mother! See what I have got because Moufflou did his tricks," he shouted. "And now you can buy those shoes you want so much, and the coffee that you miss so of a morning, and the new linen for Tasso, and the shirts for Sandro."

For to the mind of Lolo two francs was as two millions—source unfathomable of riches inexhaustible!

With the afternoon he and Moufflou trotted down the arcades of the Uffizi and down the Lung' Arno to the hotel of the stranger, and, showing the stranger's card, which Lolo could not read, they were shown at once into a great chamber, all gilding and fresco and velvet furniture.

But Lolo, being a little Florentine, was never troubled by externals, or daunted by mere sofas and chairs. He stood and looked around him with perfect composure; and Moufflou, whose attitude, when he was not romping, was always one of magisterial gravity, sat on his haunches and did the same.

Soon the foreigner he had seen in the forenoon entered and spoke to him, and led him into another chamber, where stretched on a couch was a little wan-faced boy about seven years old; a pretty boy, but so pallid, so wasted, so helpless. This poor little boy was heir to a great name and a great fortune, but all the science in the world could not make him strong enough to run about among the daisies, or able to draw a single breath without pain. A feeble smile lit up his face as he saw Moufflou and Lolo. Then a shadow chased it away.

"Little boy is lame like me," he said, in a tongue Lolo did not understand.

"Yes, but he is a strong little boy, and can move about, as perhaps the suns of his country will make you do," said the gentleman, who was the poor little boy's father. "He has brought you his poodle to amuse you. What a handsome dog, is it not?"

"Oh, *bufflins!*" said the poor little fellow, stretching out his wasted hands to Moufflou, who submitted his leonine crest to the caress.

Then Lolo went through the performance, and Moufflou acquitted himself ably as ever; and the little invalid laughed and shouted with his tiny thin voice, and enjoyed it all immensely, and rained cakes and biscuits on both the poodle and its master. Lolo crumped the pastries with willing white teeth, and Moufflou did no less. Then they got up to go, and the sick child on the couch burst into fretful lamentations and outcries.

"I want the dog! I will have the dog!" was all he kept repeating.

But Lolo did not know what he said, and was only sorry to see him so unhappy.

"You shall have the dog tomorrow," said the gentleman, to pacify his little son; and he hurried Lolo and Moufflou out of the room, and consigned them to a servant, having given Lolo five francs this time.

"Why, Moufflou," said Lolo, with a chuckle of delight, "if we could find a foreigner every day, we could eat meat at supper, Moufflou, and go to the theater every evening!"

And he and his crutch clattered home with great eagerness and excitement, and Moufflou trotted on his four frilled feet, the blue bow with which Bice had tied up his curls on the top of his head, fluttering in the wind. But, alas! even his five francs could bring no comfort at home. He found his whole family wailing and mourning in utterly inconsolable distress.

Tasso had drawn his number that morning, and the number was seven, and he must go and be a conscript for three years.

The poor young man stood in the midst of his weeping brothers and sisters, with his mother leaning against his shoulder, and down his own brown cheeks the tears were falling. He must go, and lose his place in the public gardens, and leave his people to starve as they might, and be put in a tomfool's jacket, and drafted off among cursing and swearing and strange faces, friendless, homeless, miserable! And the mother—what would become of the mother?

Tasso was the best of lads and the mildest. He was quite happy sweeping up the leaves in the long alleys of the Cascine, or mowing the green lawns under the ilex avenues, and coming home at suppertime among the merry little people and the good woman that he loved. He was quite contented; he wanted nothing, only to be let alone; and they would not let him alone. They would haul him away to put a heavy musket in his hand and a heavy knapsack on his back, and drill him, and curse him, and make him into a human target, a live popinjay.

No one had any heed for Lolo and his five francs, and Moufflou, understanding that some great sorrow had fallen on his friends, sat down and lifted up his voice and howled.

Tasso must go away!—that was all they understood. For three long years they must go without the sight of his face, the aid of his strength, the pleasure of his smile. Tasso must go! When Lolo understood the calamity that had befallen them, he gathered Moufflou up against his breast, and sat down too on the floor beside him and cried as if he would never stop crying.

There was no help for it: it was one of those misfortunes which are, as we say In Italian, like a tile tumbled on the head. The tile drops from a height, and the poor head bows under the unseen blow. That is all.

"What is the use of that?" said the mother passionately, when Lolo showed her his five francs. "It will not buy Tasso's discharge."

Lolo felt that his mother was cruel and unjust, and crept to bed with Moufflou. Moufflou always slept on Lolo's feet.

The next morning Lolo got up before sunrise, and he and Moufflou accompanied Tasso to his work in the Cascine.

Lolo loved his brother, and clung to every moment while they could still be together.

"Can nothing keep you, Tasso?" he said, despairingly, as they went down the leafy aisles, whilst the Arno water was growing golden as the sun rose.

Tasso sighed.

"Nothing, dear. Unless Gesu would send me a thousand francs to buy a substitute."

And he knew he might as well have said, "If one could coin gold ducats out of the sunbeams of Arno water."

Lolo was very sorrowful as he lay on the grass in the meadow where Tasso was at work, and the poodle lay stretched beside him.

When Lolo went home to dinner (Tasso took his wrapped in a handkerchief) he found his mother very agitated and excited. She was laughing one moment, crying the next. She was passionate and peevish, tender and jocose by turns; there was something forced and feverish about her which the children felt but did not comprehend. She was a woman of not very much intelligence, and she had a secret, and she carried it ill, and knew not what to do with it; but they could not tell that. They only felt a vague sense of disturbance and timidity at her unwonted manner.

The meal over (it was only bean soup, and that is soon eaten), the mother said sharply to Lolo. "Your aunt Anita wants you this afternoon. She has to go out, and you are needed to stay with the children: be off with you."

Lolo was an obedient child; he took his hat and jumped up as quickly as his halting hip would let him. He called Moufflou, who was asleep.

"Leave the dog," said his mother sharply. " 'Nita will not have him messing and carrying mud about her nice clean rooms. She told me so. Leave him, I say."

"Leave Moufflou!" echoed Lolo, for never in all Moufflou's life had Lolo parted from him. Leave Moufflou! He stared open-eyed and open-mouthed at his mother. What could have come to her?

"Leave him, I say," she repeated, more sharply than ever. "Must I speak twice to my own children? Be off with you, and leave the dog, I say."

And she clutched Moufflou by his long silky mane and dragged him backwards, while with the other hand she thrust out of the door Lolo and Bice.

Lolo began to hammer with his crutch at the door thus closed on him; but Bice coaxed and entreated him.

"Poor mother has been so worried about Tasso," she pleaded. "And what harm can come to Moufflou? And I do think he was tired, Lolo; the Cascine is a long way; and it is quite true that Aunt 'Nita never liked him."

So by one means and another she coaxed her brother away; and they went almost in silence to where their aunt Anita dwelt, which was across the river, near the dark-red bell-shaped dome of Santa Spirito.

It was true that her aunt had wanted them to mind her room and her babies while she was away carrying home some lace to a villa outside the Roman gate, for she was a lace-washer and clear-starcher by trade. There they had to stay in the little dark room with the two babies, with nothing to amuse the time except the clang of the bells of the church of the Holy Spirit, and the voices of the lemonade sellers shouting in the street below. Aunt Anita did not get back till it was more than dusk, and the two children trotted homeward hand in hand, Lolo's leg dragging itself painfully along, for without Moufflou's white figure dancing on before him he felt very tired indeed. It was pitch dark when they got to Or San Michele, and the lamps burned dully.

Lolo stumped up the stairs wearily, with a vague, dull fear at his small heart.

"Moufflou, Moufflou!" he called. Where was

Moufflou? Always at the first sound of his crutch the poodle came flying towards him. "Moufflou. Moufflou!" he called all the way up the long, dark twisting stone stair. He pushed open the door, and he called again, "Moufflou, Moufflou!"

But no dog answered to his call.

"Mother, where is Moufflou?" he asked, staring with blinking, dazzled eyes into the oil-lit room where his mother sat knitting. Tasso was not then home from work. His mother went on with her knitting; there was an uneasy look on her face.

"Mother, what have you done with Moufflou, *my* Moufflou?" said Lolo, with a look that was almost stern on his ten-year-old face.

Then his mother, without looking up and moving her knitting needles very rapidly, said—

"Moufflou is sold!"

And little Dina, who was a quick, pert child, cried with a shrill voice—

"Mother has sold him for a thousand francs to the foreign gentleman."

"Sold him!"

Lolo grew white and grew cold as ice; he stammered, threw up his hands over his head, gasped a little for breath, then fell down in a dead swoon, his poor useless limb doubled under him.

When Tasso came home that sad night and found his little brother shivering, moaning, and half delirious, and when he heard what had been done, he was sorely grieved.

"Oh, mother, how could you do it?" he cried. "Poor Moufflou! and Lolo loves him so!"

"I have got the money," said his mother feverishly,

"and you will not need to go for a soldier: we can buy your substitute.   What is a poodle, that you mourn about it?   We can get another poodle for Lolo."

"Another will not be Moufflou," said Tasso, and yet was seized with such a frantic happiness himself at the knowledge that he would not need go to the army, that he too felt as if he were drunk on new wine, and had not the heart to rebuke his mother.

"A thousand francs!" he muttered, "a thousand francs! *Dio mio!*   Who could ever have fancied anybody would have given such a price for a common white poodle? One would think the gentleman had bought the church and the tabernacle!"

"Fools and their money are soon parted," said his mother, with cross contempt.

It was true: she had sold Moufflou.

The English gentleman had called on her while Lolo and the dog had been in the Cascine, and had said that he was desirous of buying the poodle, which had so diverted his sick child that the little invalid would not be comforted unless he possessed it.   Now, at any other time the good woman would have sturdily refused any idea of selling Moufflou; but that morning the thousand francs which would buy Tasso's substitute were forever in her mind and before her eyes.   When she heard the foreigner her heart gave a great leap, and her head swam giddily, and she thought, in a spasm of longing—if she could get those thousand francs!   But though she was so dizzy and so upset she retained her grip on her native Florentine shrewdness.   She said nothing of her need of the money; not a syllable of her sore distress.   On the contrary, she was coy and wary, affected great reluctance to part with her pet, invented a great offer made for him by a director of a circus, and finally let fall a hint that less than a thousand francs she could never take for poor Moufflou.

The gentleman assented with so much willingness to the price that she instantly regretted not having asked double. He told her that if she would take the poodle that afternoon to his hotel the money should be paid to her; so she despatched her children after their noonday meal in various directions, and herself took Moufflou to his doom. She could not believe her senses when ten hundred franc notes were put into her hand. She scrawled her signature, Rosina Calabucci to a formal receipt, and went away, leaving Moufflou in his new owner's rooms, and hearing his howls and moans pursue her all the way down the staircase and out into the air.

She was not easy at what she had done. "It seemed," she said to herself, "like selling a Christian."

But then to keep her eldest son at home—what a joy that was! On the whole, she cried so and laughed so as she went down the Lung' Arno that once or twice people looked at her, thinking her out of her senses, and a guard spoke to her angrily.

Meanwhile, Lolo was sick and delirious with grief. Twenty times he got out of his bed and screamed to be allowed to go with Moufflou, and twenty times his mother and his brothers put him back again and held him down and tried in vain to quiet him.

The child was beside himself with misery. "Moufflou! Moufflou!" he sobbed at every moment; and by night he was in a raging fever, and when his mother, frightened, ran and called in a doctor of the quarter, that worthy shook his head and said something as to a shock of the nervous system, and muttered a long word—"meningitis."

Lolo took a hatred to the sight of Tasso, and thrust him away, and his mother too.

"It is for you Moufflou is sold," he said, with his little teeth and hands tight clinched.

After a day or two Tasso felt as if he could not bear his life, and went down to the hotel to see if the foreign gentleman would allow him to have Moufflou back for half an hour to quiet his little brother by a sight of him. But at the hotel he was told that the *Milord Inglese* who had bought the dog of Rosina Calabucci had gone that same night of the purchase to Rome, to Naples, to Palermo, *chi sa?*

"And Moufflou with him?" asked Tasso.

"The *barbone* he had bought went with him," said the porter of the hotel. "Such a beast! Howling, shrieking, raging all the day, and all the paint scratched off the *salon* door."

Poor Moufflou! Tasso's heart was heavy as he heard of that sad, helpless misery of their bartered favorite and friend.

"What matter?" said his mother fiercely, when he told her. "A dog is a dog. They will feed him better than we could. In a week he will have forgotten—*chè!*"

But Tasso feared that Moufflou would not forget. Lolo certainly would not. The doctor came to the bedside twice a day, and ice and water were kept on the aching hot little head that had got the malady with the long name, and for the chief part of the time Lolo lay quiet, dull, and stupid, breathing heavily, and then at intervals cried and sobbed and shrieked hysterically for Moufflou.

"Can you not get what he calls for to quiet him with a sight of it?" said the doctor. But that was not possible, and poor Rosina covered her head with her apron and felt a guilty creature.

"Still, you will not go to the army," she said to Tasso, clinging to that immense joy for her consolation. "Only think! We can pay Guido Squarcione to go for you. He always said he would go if anybody would pay him. Oh, my Tasso, surely to keep you is worth a dog's life!"

"And Lolo's?" said Tasso gloomily. "Nay, mother, it works ill to meddle too much with fate. I drew my number; I was bound to go. Heaven would have made it up to you somehow."

"Heaven sent me the foreigner; the Madonna's own self sent him to ease a mother's pain," said Rosina rapidly and angrily. "There are the thousand francs safe to hand in the *cassone*, and what, pray, is it we miss? Only a dog like a sheep, that brought gallons of mud in with him every time it rained, and ate as much as any one of you."

"But Lolo?" said Tasso, under his breath.

His mother was so irritated and so tormented by her own conscience that she upset all the cabbage broth into the burning charcoal.

"Lolo was always a little fool, thinking of nothing but the church and the dog and nasty field flowers," she said angrily. "I humored him ever too much because of the hurt to his hip, and so—and so——"

Then the poor soul made matters worse by dropping her tears into the saucepan, and fanning the charcoal so furiously that the flame caught her fan of cane leaves, and would have burned her arm had not Tasso been there.

"You are my prop and safety always. Who would not have done what I did? Not Santa Felicita herself," she said with a great sob.

But all this did not cure poor Lolo.

The days and the weeks of the golden autumn weather passed away, and he was always in danger, and the small, close room where he slept with Sandro and Beppo and Tasso was not one to cure such an illness as had now beset him. Tasso went to his work with a sick heart in the Cascine, where the colchicum was all lilac among the meadow grass, and the ashes and elms were taking their first flush of the coming autumnal change. He did not think Lolo would ever get well, and the good lad felt as if he had been the murderer of his little brother.

True, he had had no hand or voice in the sale of Moufflou, but Moufflou had been sold for his sake. It made him feel half guilty, very unhappy, quite unworthy all the sacrifice that had been made for him. "Nobody should meddle with fate," thought Tasso, who knew his grandfather had died in San Bonifazio because he had driven himself mad over the dream book trying to get lucky numbers for the lottery and become a rich man at a stroke.

It was rapture, indeed, to know that he was free of the army for a time at least, that he might go on undisturbed at his healthful labor, and get a raise in wages as time went on, and dwell in peace with his family, and per-haps—perhaps in time earn enough to marry pretty flaxen-haired Biondina, the daughter of the barber in the piazzetta. It was rapture indeed; but then poor Moufflou!—and poor, poor Lolo! Tasso felt as if he had bought his own exemption by seeing his little brother and the good dog torn in pieces and buried alive for his service.

And where was poor Moufflou?

Gone far away somewhere south in the hurrying, screeching, vomiting, braying train that it made Tasso giddy only to look at as it rushed by the green meadows beyond the Cascine on its way to the sea.

"If he could see the dog he cries so for, it might save him," said the doctor, who stood with grave face watching Lolo.

But that was beyond anyone's power. No one could tell where Moufflou was. He might be carried to England, to France, to Russia, to America—who could say? They did not know where his purchaser had gone. Moufflou even might be dead.

The poor mother, when the doctor said that, went and looked at the ten hundred franc notes that were once like angels' faces to her, and said to them—

"Oh, you children of Satan, why did you tempt me? I sold the poor, innocent, trustful beast to get you, and now my child is dying!"

Her eldest son would stay at home, indeed; but if this little lame one died! Rosina Calabucci would have given up the notes and consented never to own five francs in her life if only she could have gone back over the time and kept Moufflou and seen his little master running out with him into the sunshine.

More than a month went by, and Lolo lay in the same state, his yellow hair shorn, his eyes dilated and yet stupid, life kept in him by a spoonful of milk, a lump of ice, a drink of lemon water; always muttering, when he spoke at all, "Moufflou, Moufflou, *dov' è* Moufflou?" and lying for days together in somnolence and unconsciousness, with the fire eating at his brain and the weight lying on it like a stone.

The neighbors were kind, and brought fruit and the like, and sat up with him, and chattered so all at once in one continuous brawl that they were enough in themselves to kill him, for such is ever the Italian fashion of sympathy in all illness.

But Lolo did not get well, did not even seem to see the light at all, or to distinguish any sounds around him; and the doctor in plain words told Rosina Calabucci that her little boy must die. Die, and the church so near! She could not believe it. Could St. Mark, and St. George, and the rest that he had loved so do nothing for him? No, said the doctor, they could do nothing; the dog might do something, since the brain had so fastened on that one idea; but then they had sold the dog.

"Yes, I sold him!" said the poor mother, breaking into floods of remorseful tears.

So at last the end drew so nigh that one twilight time the priest came out of the great arched door that is next St. Mark, with the Host uplifted, and a little acolyte ringing the bell before it, and passed across the piazzetta, and went up the dark staircase of Rosina's dwelling, and passed through the weeping, terrified children, and went to the bedside of Lolo.

Lolo was unconscious, but the holy man touched his little body and limbs with the sacred oil, and prayed over him, and then stood sorrowful with bowed head.

Lolo had had his first communion in the summer, and in his preparation for it had shown an intelligence and devoutness that had won the priest's gentle heart.

Standing there, the holy man commended the innocent soul to God. It was the last service to be rendered to him save that very last of all when the funeral office should be read above his little grave among the millions of nameless dead at the sepulchers of the poor at Trebbiano.

All was still as the priest's voice ceased. Only the sobs of the mother and of the children broke the stillness as they knelt. The hand of Biondina had stolen into Tasso's.

Suddenly, there was a loud scuffling noise; hurrying feet came patter, patter, patter up the stairs, a ball of mud and dust flew over the heads of the kneeling figures. Fleet as the wind Moufflou dashed through the room and leaped upon the bed.

Lolo opened his heavy eyes, and a sudden light of consciousness gleamed in them like a sunbeam. "Moufflou!" he murmured, in his little thin, faint voice. The big dog pressed close to his breast and kissed his wasted face.

Moufflou was come home!

And Lolo came home, too, for death let go its hold upon him. Little by little, very faintly and flickeringly and very uncertainly at the first, life returned to the poor little body, and reason to the tormented, heated little brain. Moufflou was his physician; Moufflou, who, himself a skeleton under his matted curls, would not stir from his side and looked at him all day long with two beaming brown eyes full of unutterable love.

Lolo was happy; he asked no questions—was too weak, indeed, even to wonder. He had Moufflou; that was enough.

Alas! Though they dared not say so in his hearing, it was not enough for his elders. His mother and Tasso knew that the poodle had been sold and paid for; that they could lay no claim to keep him; and that almost certainly his purchaser would seek him out and assert his indisputable right to him. And then how would Lolo ever bear that second parting?—Lolo, so weak that he weighed no more than if he had been a little bird.

Moufflou had, no doubt, traveled a long distance and suffered much. He was but skin and bone; he bore the marks of blows and kicks; his once silken hair was all discolored and matted; he had, no doubt, traveled far. But then his purchaser would be sure to ask for him, soon or late, at his old home; and then? Well, then if they did not give him up themselves, the law would make them.

Rosina Calabucci and Tasso, though they dared say nothing before any of the children, felt their hearts in their mouth at every step on the stair, and the first interrogation of Tasso every evening when he came from his work was, "Has anyone come for Moufflou?" For ten days no one came, and their first terrors lulled a little.

On the eleventh morning, a feast day, on which Tasso was not going to his labors in the Cascine, there came a person, with a foreign look, who said the words they so much dreaded to hear: "Has the poodle that you sold to an English gentleman come back to you?"

Yes, his English master claimed him!

The servant said that they had missed the dog in Rome a few days after buying him and taking him there; that he had been searched for in vain, and that his master had thought it possible the animal might have found his way back to his old home: there had been stories of such wonderful sagacity in dogs. Anyhow, he had sent for him on the chance; he was himself back on the Lung' Arno. The servant pulled from his pocket a chain, and said his orders were to take the poodle away at once: the little sick gentleman had fretted very much about his loss.

Tasso heard in a very agony of despair. To take Moufflou away now would be to kill Lolo—Lolo so feeble still, so unable to understand, so passionately alive to every sight and sound of Moufflou, lying for hours together motionless with his hand buried in the poodle's curls, saying nothing, only smiling now and then, and murmuring a word or two in Moufflou's ear.

"The dog did come home," said Tasso, at length, in a low voice. "Angels must have shown him the road, poor beast! From Rome! Only to think of it, from Rome! And he a dumb thing! I tell you he is here, honestly: so will you not trust me just so far as this? Will you let me go with you and speak to the English lord before you take the dog away? I have a little brother sorely ill——"

He could not speak more, for tears that choked his voice.

At last the messenger agreed so far as this: Tasso might go first and see the master, but he would stay here and have a care they did not spirit the dog away—"for a thousand francs were paid for him," added the man, "and a dog that can come all the way from Rome by itself must be an uncanny creature."

Tasso thanked him, went upstairs, was thankful that his mother was at mass and could not dispute with him, took the ten hundred franc notes from the old oak *cassone,* and with them in his breast pocket walked out into the air. He was but a poor working lad, but he had made up his mind to do an heroic deed, for self-sacrifice is always heroic. He went straightway to the hotel where the English *milord* was, and when he had got there remembered that still he did not know the name of Moufflou's owner; but the people of the hotel knew him as Rosina Calabucci's son, and guessed what he wanted, and said the gentleman who had lost the poodle was within upstairs and they would tell him.

Tasso waited some half hour with his heart beating sorely against the packet of hundred franc notes. At last he was beckoned upstairs, and there he saw a foreigner with a mild fair face, and a very lovely lady, and a delicate child who was lying on a couch. "Moufflou! Where is

Moufflou?" cried the little child impatiently, as he saw the youth enter.

Tasso took his hat off and stood in the doorway an embrowned, healthy, not ungraceful figure, in his working clothes of rough blue stuff.

"If you please, most illustrious," he stammered, "poor Moufflou has come home."

The child gave a cry of delight; the gentleman and lady one of wonder. Come home! All the way from Rome!

"Yes, he has, most illustrious," said Tasso, gaining courage and eloquence, "and now I want to beg something of you. We are poor, and I drew a bad number, and it was for that my mother sold Moufflou. For myself, I did not know anything of it, but she thought she would buy my substitute, and of course she could. But Moufflou is come home, and my little brother Lolo, the little boy your most illustrious first saw playing with the poodle, fell ill of the grief of losing Moufflou, and for a month has lain saying nothing sensible, but only calling for the dog, and my old grandfather died of worrying himself mad over the lottery numbers, and Lolo was so near dying that the Blessed Host had been brought, and the holy oil had been put on him, when all at once there rushes in Moufflou, skin and bone, and covered with mud, and at the sight of him Lolo comes back to his senses, and that is now ten days ago, and though Lolo is still as weak as a newborn thing, he is always sensible, and takes what we give him to eat, and lies always looking at Moufflou and smiling, and saying, 'Moufflou, Moufflou!' and, most illustrious, I know well you have bought the dog, and the law is with you, and by the law you claim it; but I thought perhaps, as Lolo loves him so, you would let us keep the dog, and would take back the thousand francs, and myself I will go and be a soldier, and heaven will take care of them all somehow."

Then Tasso, having said all this in one breathless, monotonous recitative, took the thousand francs out of his breast pocket and held them out timidly towards the foreign gentleman, who motioned them aside and stood silent.

"Did you understand, Victor?" he said, at last, to his little son.

The child hid his face in his cushions.

"Yes, I did understand something. Let Lolo keep him; Moufflou was not happy with me."

But he burst out crying as he said it.

Moufflou had run away from him.

Moufflou had never loved him, for all his sweet cakes and fond caresses and platefuls of delicate savory meats. Moufflou had run away and found his own road over two hundred miles and more to go back to some little hungry children, who never had enough to eat themselves, and so, certainly, could never give enough to eat to the dog. Poor little boy! He was so rich and so pampered and so powerful, and yet he could never make Moufflou love him!

Tasso, who understood nothing that was said, laid the ten hundred franc notes down on a table near him.

"If you would take them, most illustrious, and give me back what my mother wrote when she sold Moufflou," he said timidly, "I would pray for you night and day, and Lolo would, too. And as for the dog, we will get a puppy and train him for your little *signorino*. They can all do tricks, more or less, it comes by nature; and as for me, I will go to the army willingly; it is not right to interfere with fate; my old grandfather died mad because he would try to be a rich man, by dreaming about it and pulling destiny by the ears, as if she were a kicking mule; only, I do pray of you, do not take away Moufflou. And to think he trotted all those miles and miles, and you carried him by train, too, and he never could have seen the road, and he had no power of speech to ask——"

Tasso broke down again in his eloquence, and drew the back of his hand across his wet eyelashes.

The English gentleman was not altogether unmoved.

"Poor faithful dog!" he said, with a sigh. "I am afraid we were very cruel to him, meaning to be kind. No, we will not claim him, and I do not think you should go for a soldier; you seem so good a lad, and your mother must need you. Keep the money, my boy, and in payment you shall train the puppy you talk of, and bring him to my little boy. I will come and see your mother and Lolo tomorrow. All the way from Rome! What wonderful sagacity! What matchless fidelity!"

You can imagine, without any telling of mine, the joy that reigned in Moufflou's home when Tasso returned thither with the money and the good tidings both. His substitute was bought without a day's delay, and Lolo rapidly recovered. As for Moufflou, he could never tell them his troubles, his wanderings, his difficulties, his perils. He could never tell them by what miraculous knowledge he had found his way across Italy, from the gates of Rome to the gates of Florence. But he soon grew plump again, and merry, and his love for Lolo was yet greater than before.

By the winter all the family went to live on an estate near Spezia that the English gentleman had purchased, and there Moufflou was happier than ever. The little English boy is gaining strength in the soft air, and he and

Lolo are great friends and play with Moufflou and the
poodle puppy half the day upon the sunny terraces and
under the green orange boughs.   Tasso is one of the
gardeners there; he will have to serve as a soldier probably
in some category or another, but he is safe for the time,
and is happy.   Lolo, whose lameness will always exempt
him from military service, when he grows to be a man
means to be a florist, and a great one.   He has learned to
read, as the first step on the road of his ambition.

"But oh, Moufflou, how *did* you find your way home?"
he asks the dog a hundred times a week.

How indeed!

No one ever knew how Moufflou had made that long
journey on foot, so many weary miles; but beyond a doubt
he had done it alone and unaided, for if anyone had
helped him they would have come home with him to claim
the reward.

And that you may not wonder too greatly at Moufflou's
miraculous journey on his four bare feet, I will add here
two facts known to friends of mine, of whose truthfulness
there can be no doubt.

One concerns a French poodle who was purchased in
Paris by the friend of my friend, and brought all the way
from Paris to Milan by train.   In a few days after his
arrival in Milan the poodle was missing; and nothing
more was heard or known of him until many weeks later
his quondam owner in Paris, on opening his door one
morning, found the dog stretched dying on the threshold
of his old home.

That is one fact; not a story, mind you, *a fact*.

The other is related to me by an Italian nobleman, who
in his youth belonged to the Guardia Nobile of Tuscany.
That brilliant corps of elegant gentlemen owned a regi-

mental pet, a poodle also, a fine merry and handsome dog of its kind; and the officers all loved and made much of him, except, alas! the commandant of the regiment, who hated him, because when the officers were on parade or riding in escort the poodle was sure to be jumping and frisking about in front of them. It is difficult to see where the harm of this was, but this odious old martinet vowed vengeance against the dog, and, being of course all powerful in his own corps, ordered the exile from Florence of the poor fellow. He was sent to a farm at Prato, twenty miles off, along the hills; but very soon he found his way back to Florence. He was then sent to Leghorn, forty miles off, but in a week's time had returned to his old comrades. He was then, by order of his unrelenting foe, shipped to the island of Sardinia. How he did it no one ever could tell, for he was carried safely to Sardinia and placed inland there in kind custody, but in some wonderful way the poor dog must have found out the sea and hidden himself on board a returning vessel, for in a month's time from his exile to the island he was back again among his comrades in Florence. Now, what I have to tell you almost breaks my heart to say, and will, I think, quite break yours to hear: alas! the brute of a commandant, untouched by such marvelous cleverness and faithfulness, was his enemy to the bitter end, and, in inexorable hatred, *had him shot!* Oh, when you grow to manhood and have power, use it with tenderness!

THE CHILD OF URBINO

*He took a jewel hung on a gold chain and threw it
over Raffaelle's shoulders*

THE CHILD OF URBINO

IT was in the year of grace 1490, in the reign of Guidobaldo, Lord of Montefeltro, Duke of Urbino—the year, by the way, of the birth of that most illustrious and gracious lady Vittoria Colonna.

It was in the spring of the year, in that mountain eyrie beloved of the Muses and coveted of the Borgia, that a little boy stood looking out of a grated casement into the calm sunshiny day. He was a pretty boy, with hazel eyes, and fair hair cut straight above his brows; he wore a little blue tunic with some embroidery about the throat of it, and had in his hand a little round flat cap of the same color. He was sad of heart this merry morning, for a dear friend of his, a friend ten years older than himself, had gone the night before on a journey over the mountains to Maestro Francesco at Bologna, there to be bound apprentice to that gentle artist. This friend, Timoteo della Vita, had been very dear to the child, had played with him and jested with him, made him toys and told him stories, and he was very full of pain at Timoteo's loss. Yet he told himself not to mind, for had not Timoteo said to him, "I go as goldsmith's 'prentice to the best of men; but I mean to become a painter"? And the child understood that to be a painter was to be the greatest and wisest the world held; he quite understood that, for he was Raffaelle, the seven-year-old son of Signor Giovanni Sanzio.

He was a very happy little boy here in this stately yet homely and kindly Urbino, where his people had come for refuge when the lances of Malatesta had ravaged and ruined their homestead. He had the dearest old grandfather in all the world; he had a loving mother, and he had a father who was very tender to him, and painted him among the angels of heaven, and was always full of pleasant conceits and admirable learning, and such true love of art that the child breathed it with every breath, as he could breathe the sweetness of a cowslip bell when he held one in his hands up to his nostrils.

It was good in those days to live in old Urbino. It was not, indeed, so brilliant a place as it became in a later day, when Ariosto came there, and Bembo and Castiglione and many another witty and learned gentleman, and the Courts of Love were held with ingenious rhyme and pretty sentiment, sad only for wantonness. But, if not so brilliant, it was homelier, simpler, full of virtue, with a wise peace and tranquillity that joined hands with a stout courage. The burgher was good friends with his prince, and knew that in any trouble or perplexity he could go up to the palace, or stop the duke in the market place, and be sure of sympathy and good counsel. There were a genuine love of beautiful things, a sense of public duty and of public spirit, a loyal temper and a sage contentment, among the good people of that time, which made them happy and prosperous.

All work was solidly and thoroughly done, living was cheap, and food good and plentiful, much better and more plentiful than it is now; in the fine old houses every stone was sound, every bit of ornament well wrought, men made their nests to live in and to pass to their children and children's children after them, and had their own fancies and their own traditions recorded in the ironwork of their casements and in the woodwork of their doors. They had their happy day of honest toil from matins bell to evensong, and then walked out or sat about in the calm evening air and looked down on the plains below that were rich with grain and fruit and woodland, and talked and laughed among each other, and were content with their own pleasant, useful lives, not burnt up with envy of desire to be someone else, as in our sickly, hurrying time most people are.

Yes, life must have been very good in those old days in old Urbino, better than it is anywhere in ours.

Can you not picture to yourself good, shrewd, wise Giovanni Sanzio, with his old father by his side, and his little son running before him, in the holy evening time of a feast day, with the deep church bells swaying above head, and the last sun rays smiting the frescoed walls, the stone bastions, the blazoned standard on the castle roof, the steep city rocks shelving down into the greenery of cheery orchard and of pear tree? I can, whenever I shut my eyes and recall Urbino as it was; and would it had been mine to live then in that mountain home, and meet that divine child going along his happy smiling way, garnering unconsciously in his infant soul all the beautiful sights and sounds around him, to give them in his manhood to the world.

"Let him alone: he will paint all this some day," said

his wise father, who loved to think that his brushes and his colors would pass in time to Raffaelle, whose hands would be stronger to hold them than his own had been. And, whether he would ever paint it or not, the child never tired of thus looking from his eyrie on the rocks and counting all that passed below through the blowing corn under the leafy orchard boughs.

There were so many things to see in Urbino in that time, looking so over the vast green valley below: a clump of spears, most likely, as men-at-arms rode through the trees; a string of market folk bringing in the produce of the orchards or the fields; perchance a red-robed cardinal on a white mule with glittering housings, behind him a sumpter train rich with baggage, furniture, gold and silver plate; maybe the duke's hunting party going out or coming homeward with caracoling steeds, beautiful hounds straining at their leash, hunting horns sounding merrily over the green country; maybe a band of free lances, with plumes tossing, steel glancing, bannerets fluttering against the sky; or maybe a quiet gray-robed string of monks or pilgrims singing the hymn sung before Jerusalem, treading the long lush grass with sandaled feet, coming towards the city, to crowd slowly and gladly up its rocky height. Do you not wish with me you could stand in the window with Raffaelle to see the earth as it was then?

No doubt the good folks of Urbino laughed at him often for a little moonstruck dreamer, so many hours did he standing looking, looking—only looking—as eyes have a right to do that see well and not altogether as others see.

Happily for him, the days of his childhood were times of peace, and he did not behold, as his father had done, the torches light up the street and the flames devour the homesteads.

At this time Urbino was growing into fame for its pottery work; those big dishes and bowls, those marriage plates and pharmacy jars, which it made, were beginning to rival the products of its neighbor Gubbio, and when its duke wished to send a bridal gift, or a present on other festal occasions, he oftenest chose some service or some rare platter of his own Urbino ware. Now, pottery had not then taken the high place among the arts of Italy that it was destined very soon to do. As you will learn when you are older, after the Greeks and the Christians had exhausted all that was beautiful in shape and substance of clay vases, the art seemed to die out, and the potters and the pottery painters died with it, or at any rate went to sleep for a great many centuries, while soldiers and prelates, nobles and mercenaries were trampling to and fro all over the land and disputing it, and carrying fire and torch, steel and desolation, with them in their quarrels and covetousness. But now, the reign of the late good duke, great Federigo, having been favorable to the Marches (as we call his province now), the potters and pottery painters, with other gentle craftsmen, had begun to look up again, and the beneficent fires of their humble ovens had begun to burn in Castel Durante, in Pesaro, in Faenza, in Gubbio, and in Urbino itself. The great days had not yet come: Maestro Giorgio was but a youngster, and Orazio Fontane not born, nor the clever baker Prestino either, nor the famous Fra Xanto; but there was a Don Giorgio even then in Gubbio, of whose work, alas! one plate now at the Louvre is all we have; and here in the ducal city on the hill rich and noble things were already being made in the stout and lustrous majolica that was destined to acquire later on so wide a ceramic fame. Jars and bowls and platters, oval dishes and ewers and basins, and big-bodied, metal-welded pharmacy vases were all made and painted at Urbino while Raffaelle Sanzio was running about on rosy infantine feet. There was a master potter of the Montefeltro at that time, one Maestro Benedetto Ronconi, whose name had not become world-renowned as Orazio Fontane's and Maestro Giorgio's did in the following century, yet in that day enjoyed the honor of all the duchy, and did things very rare and fine in the Urbino ware. He lived within a stone's throw of Giovanni Sanzio, and was a gray-haired, handsome, somewhat stern and pompous man, now more than middle-aged, who had one beauteous daughter, by name Pacifica. He cherished Pacifica well, but not so well as he cherished the things he wrought—the deep round nuptial plates and oval massive dishes that he painted with Scriptural stories and strange devices, and landscapes such as those he saw around, and flowing scrolls with Latin mottoes in black letters, and which, when thus painted, he consigned with an anxiously beating heart to the trial of the ovens, and which sometimes came forth from the trial all cracked and blurred and marred, and sometimes emerged in triumph and came into his trembling hands iridescent and lovely with those lustrous and opaline hues which we admire in them to this day as the especial glory of majolica.

Maestro Benedetto was an ambitious and vain man, and had had a hard, laborious manhood, working at his potter's wheel and painter's brush before Urbino ware was prized in Italy or even in the duchy. Now, indeed, he was esteemed at his due worth, and his work was also, and he was passably rich, and known as a good artist beyond the Marches; but there was a younger man over at Gubbio, the Don Giorgio who was precursor of unequaled Maestro Giorgio Andreoli, who surpassed him, and made him sleep o' nights on thorns, as envy makes all those to do who take her as their bedfellow.

The house of Maestro Benedetto was a long stone building, with a loggia at the back all overclimbed by hardy rose trees, and looking on a garden that was more than half an orchard, and in which grew abundantly pear trees, plum trees, and wood strawberries. The lancet windows of his workshop looked on all this quiet greenery. There were so many such pleasant workshops then in the land—calm, godly, homelike places, filled from without with song of birds and scent of herbs and blossoms. Nowadays men work in crowded, stinking cities, in close factory chambers; and their work is barren as their lives are.

The little son of neighbor Sanzio ran in and out this bigger, wider house and garden of Maestro Benedetto at his pleasure, for the maiden Pacifica was always glad to see him, and even the somber master potter would unbend to him and show him how to lay the color on to the tremulous fugitive unbaked biscuit.

Pacifica was a lovely young woman of some seventeen or eighteen summers; and perhaps Raffaelle was but remembering her when he painted in his afteryears the face of his Madonna di San Sisto. He loved her as he loved everything that was beautiful and everyone who was kind; and almost better than his own beloved father's studio, almost better than his dear old grandsire's cheerful little shop, did he love this grave, silent, sweet-smelling, sun-pierced, shadowy old house of Maestro Benedetto.

Maestro Benedetto had four apprentices or pupils in

that time learning to become *figuli,* but the one whom Raffaelle liked the most (and Pacifica, too) was one Luca Torelli, of a village above in the mountains—a youth with a noble, dark pensive beauty of his own, and a fearless gait, and a supple, tall, slender figure that would have looked well in the light coat of mail and silken doublet of a man-at-arms. In sooth, the spirit of Messer Luca was more made for war and its risks and glories than for the wheel and the brush of the bottega. But he had loved Pacifica ever since he had come down one careless holy day into Urbino, and had bound himself to her father's service in a heedless moment of eagerness to breathe the same air and dwell under the same roof as she did. He had gained little for his pains: to see her at mass and at mealtimes, now and then to be allowed to bring water from the well for her or feed her pigeons, to see her gray gown go down between the orchard trees and catch the sunlight, to hear the hum of her spinning wheel, the thrum of her viol—this was the uttermost he got of joy in two long years; and how he envied Raffaelle running along the stone floor of the loggia to leap into her arms, to hang upon her skirts, to pick the summer fruit with her, and sort with her the autumn herbs for drying!

"I love Pacifica!" he would say, with a groan, to Raffaelle. And Raffaelle would say, with a smile, "Ah, Luca, so do I!"

"It is not the same thing, my dear," sighed Luca; "I want her for my wife."

"I shall have no wife; I shall marry myself to painting," said Raffaelle, with a little grave wise face looking out from under the golden roof of his fair hair. For he was never tired of watching his father painting the saints with their branch of palm on their ground of blue or of gold, or Maestro Benedetto making the dull clay glow with angels' wings and prophets' robes and holy legends told in color.

Now, one day as Raffaelle was standing and looking thus at his favorite window in the potter's house, his friend the handsome, black-browed Luca, who was also standing there, did sigh so deeply and so deplorably that the child was startled from his dreams.

"Good Luca, what ails you?" he murmured, winding his arms about the young man's knees.

"Oh, 'Faello!" mourned the apprentice woefully. "Here is such a chance to win the hand of Pacifica if only I had talent—such talent as that Giorgio of Gubbio has! If the good Lord had only gifted me with a master's skill, instead of all this bodily strength and sinew, like a wild hog of the woods, which avails me nothing here!"

"What chance is it?" asked Raffaelle, "and what is there new about Pacifica?   She has told me nothing, and I was with her an hour."

"Dear simple one, she knows nothing of it," said Luca, heaving another tremendous sigh from his heart's deepest depths.   "You must know that a new order has come in this very forenoon from the duke; he wishes a dish and a jar of the very finest and firmest majolica to be painted with the story of Esther, and made ready in three months from this date, to then go as his gifts to his cousins of Gonzaga.   He has ordered that no cost be spared in the work, but that the painting thereof be of the best that can be produced, and the prize he will give is fifty scudi. Now, Maestro Benedetto, having known some time, it seems, of this order, has had made in readiness several large oval dishes and beautiful big-bellied jars: he gives one of each to each of his pupils—to myself, to

Berengario, to Tito, and Zenone. The master is sorely
distraught that his eyesight permits him not himself to
execute the duke's commands; but it is no secret that
should one of us be so fortunate as to win the duke's
approbation, the painter who does so shall become his
partner here and shall have the hand of Pacifica. Some
say that he has only put forth this promise as a stimulus to
get the best work done of which his bottega is capable; but
I know Maestro Benedetto too well to deem him guilty of
any such evasion. What he has said he will carry out; if
the vase and the dish win the duke's praise, they will also
win Pacifica. Now you see, 'Faello mine, why I am so
bitterly sad of heart, for I am a good craftsman enough at
the wheel and the furnace, and I like not ill the handling
and the molding of the clay, but at the painting of the clay
I am but a tyro, and Berengario or even the little Zenone
will beat me. Of that I am sure."

Raffaelle heard all this in silence, leaning his elbows on
his friend's knee, and his chin on the palms of his own
hands. He knew that the other pupils were better
painters by far than his Luca, though not one of them was
such a good-hearted or noble-looking youth, and for none
of them did the maiden Pacifica care.

"How long a time is given for the jar and the dish to be
ready?" he asked, at length.

"Three months, my dear," said Luca, with a sigh
sadder than ever. "But if it were three years, what
difference would it make? You cannot cudgel the divine
grace of art into a man with blows as you cudgel speed
into a mule, and I shall be a dolt at the end of the time as
I am now. What said your good father to me but
yesternight?—and he *is* good to me and does not despise
me. He said, 'Luca, my son, it is of no more for you to

sigh for Pacifica than for the moon. Were she mine I would give her to you, for you have a heart of gold, but Signor Benedetto will not; for never, I fear me, will you be able to decorate anything more than an apothecary's mortar or a barber's basin. If I hurt you, take it not ill; I mean kindness, and were I a stalwart youth like you I would go try my fortunes in the Free Companies in France or Spain, or down in Rome, for you are made for a soldier.' That was the best even your father could say for me, 'Faello."

"But Pacifica," said the child—"Pacifica would not wish you to join the Free Companies?"

"God knows," said Luca hopelessly. "Perhaps she would not care."

"I am sure she would," said Raffaelle, "for she does love you, Luca, though she cannot say so, being but a girl, and Signor Benedetto against you. But that redcap you tamed for her, how she loves it, how she caresses it, and half is for you, Luca, half for the bird!"

Luca kissed him.

But the tears rolled down the poor youth's face, for he was much in earnest and filled with despair.

"Even if she did, if she do," he murmured hopelessly, "she never will let me know it, since her father forbids a thought of me; and now here is this trial of skill at the duke's order come to make things worse, and if that swaggering Berengario of Fano win her, then truly will I join the free lances and pray heaven send me swift shrive and shroud."

Raffaelle was very pensive for a while; then he raised his head and said—

"I have thought of something, Luca. But I do not know whether you will let me try it."

"You angel child! What would your old Luca deny to you? But as for helping me, my dear, put that thought out of your little mind forever, for no one can help me, 'Faello, not the saints themselves, since I was born a dolt!"

Raffaello kissed him and said, "Now listen!"

A few days later Signor Benedetto informed his pupils in ceremonious audience of the duke's command and of his own intentions; he did not pronounce his daughter's name to the youths, but he spoke in terms that were clear enough to assure them that whoever had the good fortune and high merit to gain the duke's choice of his pottery should have the honor of becoming associate in his own famous bottega. Now, it had been known in Urbino ever since Pacifica had gone to her first communion that whoever pleased her father well enough to become his partner would have also to please her as her husband. Not much attention was given to maidens' wishes in those times, and no one thought the master potter either unjust or cruel in thus suiting himself before he suited his daughter. And what made the hearts of all the young men quake and sink the lowest was the fact that Signor Benedetto offered the competition not only to his own apprentices but to any native of the duchy of Urbino. For who could tell what hero might not step forth from obscurity and gain the great prize of this fair hand of Pacifica's? And with her hand would go many a broad gold ducat, and heritage of the wide old gray stone house, and many an old jewel and old brocade that were kept there in dusky sweet-smelling cabinets, and also more than one good piece of land, smiling with corn and fruit trees, outside the gates in the lower pastures to the westward.

Luca, indeed, never thought of these things, but the other three pupils did, and other youths as well. Had it not been for the limitation as to birth within the duchy, many a gallant young painter from the other side of the Apennines, many a lusty *vasalino* or *baccalino* from the workshops of fair Florence herself, or from the Lombard cities, might have traveled there in hot haste as fast as horses could carry them, and come to paint the clay for the sake of so precious a recompense. But Urbino men they had to be; and poor Luca, who was so full of despair that he could almost have thrown himself headlong from the rocks, was thankful to destiny for even so much slender mercy as this—that the number of his rivals was limited.

"Had I been you," Giovanni Sanzio ventured once to say respectfully to Signor Benedetto, "I think I should have picked out for my son-in-law the best youth that I knew, not the best painter; for be it said in all reverence, my friend, the greatest artist is not always the truest man, and by the hearthstone humble virtues have sometimes high claim."

Then Signor Benedetto had set his stern face like a flint, knowing very well what youth Messer Giovanni would have liked to name to him.

"I have need of a good artist in my bottega to keep up its fame," he had said stiffly. "My vision is not what it was, and I should be loath to see Urbino ware fall back, while Pesaro and Gubbio and Castel-Durante gain ground every day. Pacifica must pay the penalty, if penalty there be, for being the daughter of a great artist."

Mirthful, keen-witted Sanzio smiled to himself and went his way in silence; for he who loved Andrea

Mantegna did not bow down in homage before the old master potter's estimation of himself, which was in truth somewhat overweening in its vanity.

"Poor Pacifica!" he thought. "If only my 'Faello were but some decade older!"

He, who could not foresee the future, the splendid, wondrous, unequaled future that awaited his young son, wished nothing better for him than a peaceful painter's life here in old Urbino, under the friendly shadow of the Montefeltro's palace walls.

Meanwhile, where think you was Raffaelle? Half the day, or all the day, and every day whenever he could? Where think you was he? Well, in the attic of Luca, before a bowl and a dish almost as big as himself. The attic was a breezy, naked place, underneath the arches supporting the roof of Maestro Benedetto's dwelling. Each pupil had one of these garrets to himself—a rare boon, for which Luca came to be very thankful, for without it he could not have sheltered his angel; and the secret that Raffaelle had whispered to him that day of the first conference had been, "Let *me* try and paint it!"

For a long time Luca had been afraid to comply, had only forborne indeed from utter laughter at the idea from his love and reverence for the little speaker. Baby Sanzio, who was only just seven years old as the April tulips reddened the corn, painting a majolica dish and vase to go to the Gonzaga of Mantua! The good fellow could scarcely restrain his shouts of mirth at the audacious fancy; and nothing had kept him grave but the sight of that most serious face of Raffaelle, looking up to his with serene, sublime self-confidence, nay, perhaps, rather, confidence in heaven and in heaven's gifts.

"Let me try!" said the child a hundred times. He

would tell no one, only Luca would know. And if he failed—well, there would only be the spoiled pottery to pay for, and had he not two whole ducats that the duke had given him when the court had come to behold his father's designs for the altar frescoes at San Dominico di Calgi?

So utterly in earnest was he, and so intense and blank was Luca's absolute despair, that the young man had in turn given way to his entreaties. "Never can I do aught," he thought bitterly, looking at his own clumsy designs. "And sometimes by the help of cherubs the saints work miracles."

"It will be no miracle," said Raffaelle, hearing him murmur this, "it will be myself, and that which the dear God has put into me."

From that hour Luca let him do what he would, and through all these lovely early summer days the child came and shut himself up in the garret, and studied, and thought, and worked, and knitted his pretty fair brows, and smiled in tranquil satisfaction, according to the mood he was in and the progress of his labors.

Giovanni Sanzio went away at that time to paint an altarpiece over at Città di Castello, and his little son for once was glad he was absent. Messer Giovanni would surely have remarked the long and frequent visits of Raffaelle to the attic, and would, in all likelihood, have obliged him to pore over his Latin or to take exercise in the open fields; but his mother said nothing, content that he should be amused and safe, and knowing well that Pacifica loved him and would let him come to no harm under her roof. Pacifica herself did wonder that he deserted her so perpetually for the garret. But one day when she questioned him the sweet-faced rogue clung to her and murmured, "Oh, Pacifica, I do want Luca to win you, because he loves you so; and I do love you both!" And she grew pale, and answered him, "Ah, dear, if he could!" and then said never a word more, but went to her distaff; and Raffaelle saw great tears fall off her lashes down among the flax.

She thought he went to the attic to watch how Luca painted, and loved him more than ever for that, but knew in the hopelessness of her heart—as Luca also knew it in his—that the good and gallant youth would never be able to create anything that would go as the duke's gifts to the Gonzaga of Mantua. And she did care for Luca! She had spoken to him but rarely indeed, yet passing in and out of the same doors, and going to the same church offices, and dwelling always beneath the same roof, he had found means of late for a word, a flower, a serenade. And he was so handsome and so brave, and so gentle, too, and so full of deference. Poor Pacifica cared not in the least whether he could paint or not. He could have made her happy.

In the attic Raffaelle passed the most anxious hours of all his sunny little life. He would not allow Luca even to look at what he did. He barred the door and worked; when he went away he locked his work up in a wardrobe. The swallows came in and out of the unglazed window, and fluttered all around him; the morning sunbeams came in too, and made a nimbus round his golden head, like that which his father gilded above the heads of saints. Raffaelle worked on, not looking off, though clang of trumpet, or fanfare of cymbal, often told him there was much going on worth looking at down below. He was only seven years old, but he labored as earnestly as if he were a man grown, his little rosy fingers gripping that pencil which was to make him in life and death famous as kings are not famous, and let his tender body lie in its last sleep in the Pantheon of Rome.

He had covered hundreds of sheets with designs before he had succeeded in getting embodied the ideas that haunted him. When he had pleased himself at last, he set to work to transfer his imaginations to the clay in color in the subtle luminous metallic enamel that characterizes Urbino majolica.

Ah, how glad he was now that his father had let him draw from the time he was two years old, and that of late Messer Benedetto had shown him something of the mysteries of painting on biscuit and producing the metallic luster which was the especial glory of the pottery of the duchy!

How glad he was, and how his little heart bounded and seemed to sing in this his first enjoyment of the joyous liberties and powers of creative work!

A well-known writer has said that genius is the power of taking pains; he should have said rather that genius *has* this power also, but that first and foremost it possesses the power of spontaneous and exquisite production without effort and with delight.

Luca looked at him (not at his work, for the child had made him promise not to do so) and began to marvel at his absorption, his intentness, the evident facility with which he worked. The little figure, leaning over the great dish on the bare board of the table, with the oval opening of the window and the blue sky beyond it, began to grow sacred to him with more than the sanctity of childhood. Raffaelle's face grew very serious, too, and lost its color, and his large hazel eyes looked very big and grave and dark.

"Perhaps Signor Giovanni will be angry with me if ever he knows," thought poor Luca, but it was too late to alter anything now. The child Sanzio had become his master.

So Raffaelle, unknown to anyone else, worked on and on there in the attic while the tulips bloomed and withered, and the honeysuckle was in flower in the hedges, and the wheat and barley were being cut in the quiet fields lying far down below in the sunshine. For midsummer was come; the three months all but a week had passed by. It was known that everyone was ready to compete for the duke's choice.

One afternoon Raffaelle took Luca by the hand and said to him, "Come."

He led the young man up to the table, beneath the unglazed window, where he had passed so many of these ninety days of the spring and summer.

Luca gave a great cry, and stood gazing, gazing, gazing. Then he fell on his knees and embraced the little feet of the child: it was the first homage that he, whose life became one beautiful song of praise, received from man.

"Dear Luca," he said softly, "do not do that. If it be indeed good, let us thank God."

What his friend saw were the great oval dish and the great jar or vase standing with the sunbeams full upon them, and the brushes and the tools and the colors all strewn around. And they shone with lustrous opaline hues and wondrous flame-like glories and gleaming iridescence, like melted jewels, and there were all manner of graceful symbols and classic designs wrought upon them; and their borders were garlanded with cherubs and flowers, bearing the arms of Montefeltro, and the landscapes were the tender, homely landscapes round about

Urbino; and the mountains had the solemn radiance that the Apennines wore at evening time, and amidst the figures there was one supreme, white-robed, golden-crowned Esther, to whom the child painter had given the face of Pacifica. And this wondrous creation, wrought by a baby's hand, had safely and secretly passed the ordeal of the furnace, and had come forth without spot or flaw.

Luca ceased not from kneeling at the feet of Raffaelle, as ever since has kneeled the world.

"Oh, wondrous boy! Oh, angel sent unto men!" sighed the poor 'prentice, as he gazed and his heart was so full that he burst into tears.

"Let us thank God," said little Raffaelle again; and he joined his small hands that had wrought this miracle, and said his Laus Domini.

When the precious jar and the platter were removed to the wardrobe and shut up in safety behind the steel wards of the locker, Luca said, timidly, feeling twenty years in age behind the wisdom of this divine child, "But, dearest boy, I do not see how your marvelous and most exquisite accomplishment can advantage me. Even if you would allow it to pass as mine, I could not accept such a thing: it would be a fraud, a shame: not even to win Pacifica could I consent."

"Be not so hasty, good friend," said Raffaelle. "Wait just a little longer yet and see. I have my own idea. Do trust in me."

"Heaven speaks in you, that I believe," said Luca humbly.

Raffaelle answered not, but ran downstairs, and passing Pacifica, threw his arms about her in more than his usual affectionate caresses.

"Pacifica, be of good heart," he murmured, and would not be questioned, but ran homeward to his mother.

"Can it be that Luca has done well?" thought Pacifica; but she feared the child's wishes had outrun his wisdom. He could not be any judge, a child of seven years, even though he were the son of that good and honest painter and poet Giovanni Sanzio.

The next morning was midsummer day. Now, the pottery was all to be placed on this forenoon in the bottega of Signor Benedetto; and the Duke Guidobaldo was then to come and make his choice from amidst them; and the master potter, a little because he was a courtier, and more because he liked to affect a mighty indifference and to show he had no favoritism, and declared that he would not himself see the competing works of art until the eyes of the Lord of Montefeltro also fell upon them.

As for Pacifica, she had locked herself in her chamber, alone with her intense agitation. The young men were swaggering about, and taunting each other, and boasting. Luca alone sat apart, thrumming an old lute. Giovanni Sanzio, who had ridden home at evening from Città di Castello, came in from his own house and put his hand on the youth's shoulder.

"I hear the Pesaro men have brought fine things. Take courage, my lad. Maybe we can entreat the duke to dissuade Pacifica's father from this tyrannous disposal of her hand."

Luca shook his head wearily.

There would be one beautiful thing there, indeed, he knew; but what use would that be to him?

"The child—the child——" he stammered, and then remembered that he must not disclose Raffaelle's secret.

"My child?" said Signor Giovanni. "Oh, he will be

here; he will be sure to be here. Wherever there is a painted thing to be seen, there always, be sure, is Raffaelle."

Then the good man sauntered within from the loggia, to exchange salutations with Ser Benedetto, who, in a suit of fine crimson with doublet of sand-colored velvet, was standing ready to advance bareheaded into the street as soon as the hoofs of the duke's charger should strike on the stones.

"You must be anxious in your thoughts," said Signor Giovanni to him. "They say a youth from Pesaro brings something fine: if you should find yourself bound to take a stranger into your workroom and your home——"

"If he be a man of genius he will be welcome," answered Messer Ronconi pompously. "Be he of Pesaro, or of Fano, or of Castel-Durante, I go not back from my word. I keep my word, to my own hindrance even, ever."

"Let us hope it will bring you only joy and triumph here," said his neighbor, who knew him to be an honest man and a true, if overobstinate and too vain of his own place in Urbino.

"Our lord the duke!" shouted the people standing in the street and Ser Benedetto walked out with stately tread to receive the honor of his master's visit to his bottega.

Raffaelle slipped noiselessly up to his father's side, and slid his little hand into Sanzio's.

"You are not surely afraid of our good Guidobaldo!" said his father, with a laugh and some little surprise, for Raffaelle was very pale, and his lower lip trembled a little.

"No," said the child simply.

The young duke and his court came riding down the

street, and paused before the old stone house of the
master potter—splendid gentlemen, though only in their
morning apparel, with noble Barbary steeds fretting
under them, and little pages and liveried varlets about
their steps. Usually, unless he went hunting or on a visit
to some noble, Guidobaldo, like his father, walked about
Urbino like any one of his citizens; but he knew the
pompous and somewhat vainglorious temper of Messer
Benedetto, and good-naturedly was willing to humor its
harmless vanities. Bowing to the ground, the master
potter led the way, walking backward into his bottega; the
courtiers followed their prince; Giovanni Sanzio with his
little son and a few other privileged persons went in also
at due distance. At the farther end of the workshop stood
the pupils and the artists from Pesaro and other places in
the duchy whose works were there in competition. In all
there were some ten competitors: poor Luca, who had set
his own work on the table with the rest as he was obliged
to do, stood hindmost of all, shrinking back, to hide his
misery, into the deepest shadow of the deep-bayed latticed window.

On the narrow deal benches that served as tables on
working days to the pottery painters were ranged the
dishes and the jars, with a number attached to each—no
name to any, because Signor Benedetto was resolute to
prove his own absolute disinterestedness in the matter of
choice: he wished for the best artist. Prince Guidobaldo,
doffing his plumed cap courteously, walked down the long
room and examined each production in its turn. On the
whole, the collection made a brave display of majolica,
though he was perhaps a little disappointed at the result in
each individual case, for he had wanted something out of
the common run and absolutely perfect. Still, with fair

words he complimented Signor Benedetto on the brave show, and only before the work of poor Luca was he entirely silent, since indeed silence was the greatest kindness he could show to it: the drawing was bold and regular, but the coloring was hopelessly crude, glaring, and ill disposed.

At last, before a vase and a dish that stood modestly at the very farthest end of the deal bench, the duke gave a sudden exclamation of delight, and Signor Benedetto grew crimson with pleasure and surprise, and Giovanni Sanzio pressed a little nearer and tried to see over the shoulders of the gentlemen of the court, feeling sure that something rare and beautiful must have called forth that cry of wonder from the Lord of Montefeltro, and having seen at a glance that for his poor friend Luca there was no sort of hope.

"This is beyond all comparison," said Guidobaldo, taking the great oval dish up reverently in his hands. "Maestro Benedetto, I do felicitate you indeed that you should possess such a pupil. He will be a glory to our beloved Urbino."

"It is indeed most excellent work, my lord duke," said the master potter, who was trembling with surprise and dared not show all the astonishment and emotion that he felt at the discovery of so exquisite a creation in his bottega. "It must be," he added, for he was a very honest man, "the work of one of the lads of Pesaro or Castel-Durante. I have no such craftsman in my workshop. It is beautiful exceedingly!"

"It is worth its weight in gold!" said the prince, sharing his emotion. "Look, gentlemen—look! Will not the fame of Urbino be borne beyond the Apennines and Alps?"

Thus summoned, the court and the citizens came to look, and averred that truly never in Urbino had they seen such painting on majolica.

"But whose is it?" said Guidobaldo, impatiently, casting his eyes over the gathered group in the background of apprentices and artists. "Maestro Benedetto, I pray you, the name of the artist; I pray you, quick!"

"It is marked number eleven, my lord," answered the master potter. "Ho, you who reply to that number, stand out and give your name. My lord duke has chosen your work. Ho, there! do you hear me?"

But not one of the group moved. The young men looked from one to another. Who was this nameless rival? There were but ten of themselves.

"Ho, there!" repeated Signor Benedetto, getting angry. "Cannot you find a tongue, I say? Who has wrought this work? Silence is insolence to his highness and to me!"

Then the child Sanzio loosened his little hand from his father's hold, and went forward, and stood before the master-potter.

"I painted it," he said, with a pleased smile. "I, Raffaelle."

Can you not fancy, without telling, the confusion, the wonder, the rapture, the incredulity, the questions, the wild ecstasy of praise, that followed on the discovery of the child artist? Only the presence of Guidobaldo kept it in anything like decent quietude, and even he, all duke though he was, felt his eyes wet and felt his heart swell; for he himself was childless, and for the joy that Giovanni Sanzio felt that day he would have given his patrimony and duchy.

He took a jewel hung on a gold chain from his own breast and threw it over Raffaelle's shoulders.

"There is your first guerdon," he said. "You will have many, O wondrous child, who shall live when we are dust!"

Raffaelle, who himself was all the while quite tranquil and unmoved, kissed the duke's hand with sweetest grace, then turned to his own father.

"It is true I have won my lord duke's prize?"

"Quite true, my angel!" said Giovanni Sanzio, with tremulous voice.

Raffaelle looked up at Maestro Benedetto.

"Then I claim the hand of Pacifica!"

There was a smile on all the faces round, even on the darker countenances of the vanquished painters.

"Oh, would indeed you were of age to be my son by marriage, as you are the son of my heart!" murmured Signor Benedetto. "Dear and marvelous child, you are but jesting, I know. Tell me what it is indeed that you would have. I could deny you nothing; and truly it is you who are my master."

"I am your pupil," said Raffaelle, with that pretty, serious smile of his, his little fingers playing with the ducal jewel. "I could never have painted that majolica yonder had you not taught me the secrets and management of your colors. Now, dear maestro mine, and you, O my lord duke, do hear me! I by the terms of the contest have won the hand of Pacifica and the right of association with Messer Ronconi. I take these rights and I give them over to my dear friend Luca of Fano, because he is the honestest man in all the world, and does honor Signor Benedetto and love Pacifica as no other can do so well, and Pacifica loves him; and my lord duke will say that thus all will be well."

So with the grave innocent audacity of a child he

spoke—this seven-year-old painter who was greater than any there.

Signor Benedetto stood mute, somber, agitated. Luca had sprung forward and dropped on one knee. He was as pale as ashes. Raffaelle looked at him with a smile.

"My lord duke," he said, with his little gentle smile, "you have chosen my work; defend me in my rights."

"Listen to the voice of an angel, my good Benedetto; heaven speaks by him," said Guildobaldo gravely, laying his hand on the arm of his master potter.

Harsh Signor Benedetto burst into tears.

"I can refuse him nothing," he said, with a sob. "He will give such glory unto Urbino as never the world hath seen!"

"And call down this fair Pacifica whom Raffaelle has won," said the sovereign of the duchy, "and I will give her myself as her dower as many gold pieces as we can cram into this famous vase. An honest youth who loves her and whom she loves—what better can you do, Benedetto? Young man, rise up and be happy. An angel has descended on earth this day for you."

But Luca heard not. He was still kneeling at the feet of Raffaelle, where the world has knelt ever since.

MELEAGRIS GALLOPAVO

He kept up side by side with the pig

MELEAGRIS GALLOPAVO

A TURKEY stood on a wall and saw a drove of black and gray pigs go by on the highroad underneath. The turkey was a very handsome gobbler, and his plumage was of the most brilliant gray and white, and his wattles were of the red of the carnation or the rose. He was very proud, and as he looked down on the pigs he stuck up his tail peacock-wise and fanned the air with it, and strutted up and down on the stone ledge, and said to himself, "What poor, dusty, hard-driven drudges those are in the road there! And not a single feather upon them! Nothing to cover their bodies except a few dingy-looking hairs! And they can only make an odd snuffling noise instead of gobbling! What a contemptible grunting and grumbling! And then what a tail!—a wisp of rope would be better!"

Then he spread his own tail higher and higher and broader and broader, just to show the pigs what a tail could be; and he gobbled loudly, that they might know what intelligible and melodious speech was like.

The poor pigs went snuffling and shuffling along in the mud and stones beneath the wall, and were driven into the straw yard of the turkey's own farmhouse.

Next morning, lo! the turkey was put in a coop and was carried off to market, with a number of ducks and geese and cackling pullets, and who should be next to him but a poor gray pig, with his heels tied together so that he could not stir.

"What a wretched creature!" said the turkey in its pride, for the coop had not taken down its vanity one peg. "What a sorry animal! and such a tail! Of course they are going to cut his throat. As for me, this is a throne: I suppose I am going to the palace. Perhaps the queen has never seen a beautiful turkey before."

Then he began again to spread out his tail-plume and shake his rosy wattles, and began to gobble, gobble, gobble with all his might. But the cart gave a lurch and the coop tilted on one side, and the turkey tilted up with it and lost his balance.

"Dear me! what a price one pays for being of high rank in this world!" he said to himself, as he clung to the side of the wicker-work and tried to preserve his dignity.

The poultry were all in flat baskets, and so were the geese and the ducks.

"He'll be fine for killing three months hence, ma'am!" his driver was saying as he stopped the cart and held up the coop to show our gentleman to a woman who stood on the curbstone.

"For killing!" echoed the turkey, and he swooned away, and fell in a heap of ruffled feathers on the bottom of the wicker-work prison.

For death had never occurred to him as a possible fate for himself, though he saw other creatures go daily to martyrdom.

"You will be sooner or later killed, just as I shall be," said the pig, with a grunt, as the turkey came to itself.

"What do you suppose they fatten you for? For love of you? Ugh! you silly vain thing!"

"I thought it was because—because—because I am a turkey!" sighed the poor prisoner in the coop.

"Because you are a turkey!" echoed the pig. "As if there were not five hundred thousand turkeys in the world! That is all. You will be before Christmas just as I shall be: a knife will slit your throat."

The poor turkey swooned again on hearing this, and did not recover so rapidly as before; therefore the cart had jolted on again and was standing in the market-place, with the horses out of the shafts, before he opened his eyes and regained his consciousness.

The master of the cart was away from it, and it had been unpacked of most of its contents, and the pig and the turkey were left alone.

Suddenly the pig gave a grunt, and the turkey started, for his nerves were on edge and the least thing frightened him.

"What a hideous voice you have!" he said pettishly. "You should hear *me!*"

And he began to gobble with all his might.

"I don't see that your noise is a bit prettier than mine," said the pig. "But it is very silly to lose your time squabbling about voices. We could get out if you would help me a little."

The turkey was silent.

To get out would be delightful; but to go into partnership with piggy hurt his pride so much that he would not even ask in what way escape could be accomplished. But the pig was in too much haste and too much in earnest to stand upon etiquette.

"I can get my snout to your coop," he said eagerly,

"and I will gnaw it asunder—it's nothing but wicker—if you will promise to peck my cords to pieces when you are out. Now, don't you see what I mean?"

The turkey was so enraptured that his pride all tumbled down like a broken egg, and his wings began to flap in a tremendous flurry.

"Make haste! make haste!" he cried, and gobbled till he was red in the face.

"Don't make such a noise, or they'll hear you," said the pig, getting his teeth well onto the wicker, "and then you and I shall go up as the alderman and his chains on to some horrid man's table."

"Alderman?" said the turkey.

"They call a roast turkey and its sausages so," explained the pig.

The turkey thought it very ghastly pleasantry.

The pig meanwhile was hard at work, and in a very little time he had gnawed, and pulled, and bitten, and twisted the coop on the side near to him in such an effectual manner that the turkey soon got his head through, and then his throat, and then his body. He gave a gobble of glory and joy.

"But undo me!" squeaked the pig.

Now, the turkey was in a fearful hurry to be gone; his heart beat and his wings flapped so that he almost fell into convulsions; but he was a bird of honor and good faith. He bent down and pecked with such frantic force at the knots tying the pig's legs that he filled his beak with frayed cord, and in less time than I take to write it piggy tumbled in his heavy fashion off the cart on to the ground—free.

"Now run," said the pig; and nobody knows how fast a pig can run who has not seen him put his mind and his will into it. The turkey could not fly, because his wings were cut, and tame turkeys seldom know much about flying; but, what with a stride and a flutter mixed in one, he managed to cover the ground rapidly, and kept up side by side with the pig, who, for his part, knowing the country, kept steadily on down the road, which fortunately for them was a solitary one, and made straight for a wood which he saw in the distance. The wood was about a mile and a half off, and the two comrades were in sore distress when they came up to it; but they did reach it unstopped, and sank down on the grass under some larches with a sigh of content.

"Such a useless tree the larch!" murmured the pig; "not an acorn on it once in all its days!" For, of course, the pig viewed all trees only in relation to acorns.

"I can't eat acorns," sighed the turkey, as soon as he got his breath.

"You ungrateful creature," said the pig in reproof. "Be content that you have escaped with your life."

"Are you *sure* we have escaped?"

"We have escaped for the time," said the philosophic pig, "and to be loose in a wood is heaven upon earth. There must be grain, or berries, or something you can pick up, if only you will look about for it."

Now it was easy for the good pig to be philosophic, because near at hand he had smelled out a savory spot in the mossy ground, and he was right in the very middle of a hearty meal of truffles.

"I never thought to have to beg my bread," sighed the turkey.

"Who do you suppose would take the trouble to feed you if it was not to kill you?" grunted the pig, with his mouth quite full. "You need not *beg* your bread, as you call it; *look* for it—as I do."

The turkey, pressed by hunger, did begin to look. A tame turkey, you know, knows nothing about feeding itself; food is thrown out to it; and our turkey, at any rate, had always supposed that was an ordination of Providence.

But little by little, watching the pig devouring the truffles, natural appetites and instincts awoke in him. No doubt his grandparents a hundred times removed had been wild turkeys by the borders of the Missouri or in the woods of Arkansas, and hereditary instincts revived in him under the all-potent prick of hunger. He did begin to look about, and spied a wild strawberry or two and ate them, and saw a blackberry bush and stripped it, and, finding a big grasshopper and a small frog, found an appetite also for them.

"I never knew so much natural nourishment grew about one," he remarked to the pig, who snorted—

"There is food enough; only men take it all. Your people are all in America, but men can't let them alone even there, so I have heard. Oh, there is a pretty hen pheasant! Good morning, Madame Phasiani."

"Is that her name?" asked the turkey.

"It is her family name; and your own is Meleagris Gallopavo, and I don't suppose you knew that," said the pig very snappishly.

The turkey was silent. Meleagris Gallopavo! That really was a very fine name!

"Is one well off in this wood, Madame Phasiani?" asked the pig of the pheasant, who sighed, and replied that the wood was very nice, and Indian corn was thrown out twice a day; but then when there was the trail of the beater over it all, who could be happy?

"There is the trail of the butcher over me," said the pig,

"but I enjoy myself while I can. You mentioned Indian corn, madame. Is the keeper's cottage unfortunately near us, then?"

She said it was perhaps half a mile off.

"This is a preserve, then?" said the pig.

She sighed again, and said it was, and sauntered pensively away with her head on one side, as pheasants always do.

"I hoped it was a bit of wild coppice," said the pig. "Ah, here is a kingfisher. How do, Mr. Alced?"

But the kingfisher, who is the shyest creature upon earth, skimmed away in silence.

"Why do you call them all those fine names?" said the turkey.

"It costs nothing, and it pleases them," said the pig curtly. "It is part of men's tomfoolery," he added, after a pause; and then, seeing a turtledove, he grunted in his most amiable fashion, "Sir Turtur Auritus, good day. We are resting in your wood a little while; it is very cool, and green, and pleasant. May I ask if it be also *safe?*"

"Safe!" said the turtledove, sitting down on a cranberry bough. "There are guns, guns, guns, from morning to night."

"Surely not this time of the year? No!"

"There are for us," said the turtledove sorrowfully, "and when there are not guns there are traps. They have no mercy on us. We only eat the pine kernels, the wood spurge, grain, the little snails. We do no harm. Yet they hunt us down; they put poisoned colza for us; they kill us by thousands; and I have heard—though it seems too terrible to be true—that they pack us alive in hampers, keep us shut up one atop of another for days, then pull our tail feathers out, and shut us up again in another box; when that box flies open they shoot at us, so I have heard."

"Oh, yes; my gentlemen call that their *'poules,'* and give each other prizes for doing it," said the pig, with a grim sympathy. "They think it vulgar when the lads at village fairs grease our tails and hunt us. Dear Sir Turtur Auritus, is there such a gigantic sham, such an unutterable beast anywhere as Man?"

"I should think there is not," said the turtledove. "Myself I live out of the world, on the top of that lime tree you see there, and if I can only alight safely to feed and drink twice a day, I ask no more."

A pretty partridge went tripping by at that moment, with some finely grown sons and daughters after her. She was a charming and lovely creature, only she had a sadly nervous manner.

"When it grows near the first of September," she said in a tone of apology to the pig, who saluted her as Lady Starnacineria, "every sound, the very slightest, sends my heart up into my mouth, and I take every stone for a dog. What is the use or the joy of bringing these dear children into a world of shot? Their doom is to be huddled alive into a game bag, with broken limbs and torn bodies, and my lord will think himself a saint fit for heaven if he send a hamper of them up to a hospital."

"All men's hypocrisy, madame," said the pig. "I prefer the frank, blunt snap of the fox, who makes no pretense of Christian charity, but only wants his dinner."

"If it were only the fox," sighed the partridge, "that would be very bearable; and he likes a common hen quite as well as ourselves—and better, because the poor vulgar creature is bigger."

With a sigh she devoted herself to laying open an ants' nest, and called to her young to devour the eggs in it.

"This seems a very nice home of yours," said the pig, to provoke conversation.

The partridge sighed as the pheasant had done.

"It is too charming among these turnips," she said, "and there is most excellent fare all over these fields; but, alas! for what a fate do I live and hatch these dear children—the gun, the dog, the bag! Ah, dear sir, life to a partridge, where man is, is only a vale of tears, though led in the best of cornfields!"

And she said, "Cheep, cheep," and made a restless little flutter of all her feathers, and crept under the rail again back among the turnips.

At that moment a fine black rabbit, with a white tuft for a tail, darted by too quick for the pig to stop him.

"Ah, he has a sad life—almost as sad as mine!" said the turtledove. "He dwells in quite a humble way underground, but they never let him alone. When they can shoot nothing else, they are forever banging and blazing at him. And they put a ferret through his hall door without even knocking to say they are there. Have you ever seen the poor bunnies sitting outside their warrens cleaning their faces like pussycats in the cool of the early morning! Ah, such a pretty sight! But men only want them for their pelts or to put them in a pie."

"What is your opinion of men, dear lady?" said the pig, as a cow came and looked over the fence.

"Oh, don't mention them!" said the cow, with unfeigned horror. "Don't they massacre all my pretty children, and drive me to market with my udders bursting, and break my heart and brand my skin? And when I am grown old will they not knock me on the head, or run a knife through my spine, and turn me into a hundred uses, hide, and hoofs, and everything? It is all written in their children's lesson books. 'The most useful animal in the kingdom of nature is a cow.' That is what they say. Ugh!"

"My dear friend," said the pig, turning to the turkey, "you see that every living thing is devoured by man. Why should you suppose you were to be the exception?"

"No one has such a tail as I have," said the turkey.

His fright over, he had come to the conclusion that nobody would ever do anything except adore a being with such a tail as his.

"What is your tail compared with the peacock's?" said the pig, with scorn. "You are only so vain because you are so ignorant."

"Do they kill peacocks?" asked the turkey.

"No; I don't think they do," replied the pig, truthful, though truth demolished his theories, which is more than can be said for human philosophers.

"Then why do they keep them?" said the turkey.

"Because they have such wonderful tails," said the pig incautiously.

"There!" said the turkey triumphantly; and out he spread his own tail, making it into a very grand wheel, and crying with all his might in that peculiar voice which nature has given to turkeys, "I am Meleagris Gallopavo! I am Meleagris Gallopavo!"

He had never known his new name till five minutes previously; but that made no difference: he was just as vain of it as if he had borne it all his life. Ask the Herald's College if this be uncommon.

He had stretched his throat out, and his rosy wattles glowed like geraniums, and he turned slowly round and round so that everyone might admire him, and he stuck his tail up on high as stiff and as straight as if it had been made of pasteboard.

"I am Meleagris Gallopavo!" he cried, with a very shrill shriek, and scattered the sandy soil of the wood all about him with his hind claws.

Crack! A bludgeon rolled him over, a mere ball of ruffled, crumpled feathers, on the ground, and a lurcher dog ran into him and gripped him tight and hard.

"We're in luck, mate!" said an ill-looking fellow who was prowling along the edge of the field with another as ill favored. "Mum's the word, and he'll go in the pot worth twenty rabbits. Who'd ha' thought of finding a darned turkey out on the spree?"

Then the cruel man rammed poor Meleagris Gallopavo into a bag that he carried with him. He was a village ne'er-do-weel, seeing if he could trespass with impunity and knock over a bunny or two on the sly, knowing that the keepers were away from that part of the wood that day. The pig lay hidden among the wood spurge and the creeping moss, and looked so exactly like a log of grayish brown timber that the ruffians never noticed him.

"I knew his tail would be the undoing of him!" he said sorrowfully, as his poor friend was borne off dead in the poachers' sack.

He himself had never looked so complacently on his own gray hairless wisp as he did now. How convenient it was! Anybody would take it for a bit of dry grass or a twig.

I may as well add that the mistress of the wood came through it next day, and the pig followed her home, and ate an apple which she gave him so cannily that she sent him into her yard, and has kept him like a very prince of pigs ever since.   But he is always sorry for his poor friend's fate; and he has never since told any turkey that its family name is Meleagris Gallopavo.